THE TYCOON AND THE SCHOOLTEACHER

•

Ludima Gus Burton

AVALON BOOKS
NEW YORK

© Copyright 2000 by Ludima Gus Burton
Library of Congress Catalog Card Number: 00-102196
ISBN 0-8034-9432-7
All rights reserved.
All the characters in this book are fictitious,
and any resemblance to actual persons,
living or dead, is purely coincidental.
Published by Thomas Bouregy & Co., Inc.
160 Madison Avenue, New York, NY 10016

PRINTED IN THE UNITED STATES OF AMERICA
ON ACID-FREE PAPER
BY HADDON CRAFTSMEN, BLOOMSBURG, PENNSYLVANIA

Dedicated to my family and writing friends for their encouragement and constant support.

Chapter One

Five miles from the Adirondack Mountain city of Canfield, the rust-pocked, ancient car, with its rattles and squeaks, inched its way down the drive to the east of the mansion house. It coasted down a hill to come to a shuddering stop in the parking area before a row of buildings.

The annoying, grating noises brought Alexander Stone and his head mechanic to the shadowed doorway of a garage.

With a hard push on the car door, Brenda Harrison swung out her legs. She reached in and grabbed a black briefcase. Taking a deep breath, she pulled at her suit coat to straighten it. With her gaze on the uneven, flagstone walk, she started toward the first building.

"She can't be the writer Uncle Charles hired for me," Alexander Stone muttered to his mechanic. "I should have found the time to do it myself." He took a deep breath. "She's too . . . too . . ." For once in his life, Alexander was at a loss for words.

The sun gleamed on her straight black hair which was parted in the middle and drawn back over the tops of her small ears to form a tight bun at the nape of her slender neck. Her black suit was buttoned over a high-necked, white blouse. The coat emphasized her small waist and flared over pleasing, generous hips. A straight skirt swept the upper calves of eye-catching legs. Her dark-rimmed glasses conjured up uneasy memories of his old English teacher.

"Hello, I'm Brenda Harrison." Her radiant smile crinkled the lines at the corners of her eyes and deepened the dimple in her left cheek. It washed over Alexander with all its charm. "Please direct me to Mr. Alexander Stone. He's expecting me."

No, Alexander wanted to answer her, you definitely aren't what I expected. She was supposed to be a middle-aged and pleasantly dowdy schoolteacher. Certainly not one who wears three-inch heels that are so out of character with the rest of her persona.

He fought the attraction of the smile and the way her face lit up. His first impression of the woman was that she couldn't be the writer he would have hired. But, if she had smiled at Uncle Charles as she just had at him, he could understand why she had been hired.

But he didn't need to keep her.

The Tycoon and the Schoolteacher   3

He stepped out of the garage doorway. "I'm Alexander Stone."

Brenda hid her surprise. Pictures of thirty-five-year-old Alexander Stone in the tabloids and magazines hadn't prepared her for a sun-bronzed Viking, with rumpled hair of streaked blond and a promise of rock-hard muscles under the thin, ragged T-shirt.

Faded jeans hugged his thighs. A fine coating of golden hair covered the bare forearms and the backs of his hands. A straight nose, a hard, square jaw and deep-set gray eyes completed the near perfect composition. Unsmiling, he looked threatening, dangerous—and cold.

Another picture came to mind. He was the Greek god Apollo, the American version, come to life in front of her—but in stone, like his name.

"Please come with me," he said, turning away abruptly. He walked with long strides to the first building and into a small corner office.

Brenda gave a quick hop to fall into step.

Before entering the office, she glanced at the rows of vintage cars which filled the rest of the long building. For the first time, she began to realize the formidable task she had lightly taken upon herself. Would she be able to do it?

Her new employer motioned for her to sit down. He took the chair behind the cluttered desk.

"What exactly is your arrangement with my uncle?"

"He asked me to write a book on your family's collection of vintage cars which you want to give to your

4 *Ludima Gus Burton*

parents for their anniversary. I'll have two months this summer to do it." She didn't know whether she should mention the offered salary which had almost caused her to hyperventilate.

"Did you bring the résumé you submitted to him? What books have you written? Do you have a written contract for this book? An advance—" He fired the questions at her.

"Wait a minute!" Brenda protested. Taking a deep breath, she answered, "I . . . I haven't written any books and I don't have a contract . . . nor did I get an advance from Charles Stone." She stopped to gather her thoughts. At the interview last week she had voiced her inexperience, but Charles Stone had brushed her fears aside.

"I have been, however, a high school teacher of English for five years. Since I teach my students how to write, your uncle was confident I could write this little book."

Little book! Alexander's intent gaze flashed with displeasure. He wanted the best book possible to give to his parents. Who was this woman making light of his proposal? She had to go. Obviously she was no serious writer.

Alexander opened his mouth—then closed it. He couldn't hurt his uncle's feelings after he had helped him out in this busy season. A year ago, his brush with death in a race-car accident had forced him to give up racing. He'd come home to pick up his over-

The Tycoon and the Schoolteacher 5

due responsibilities in running his family's luxury car business.

"I suggest a trial period of one month to see how we work together," Alexander said.

Brenda lifted her head and looked Alexander in the eyes. His manner made her think of a god on a throne, dispensing his favor on her. She had two university degrees and was an experienced teacher, so she'd make sure she lasted more than the month he so ungraciously offered.

Brenda longed to walk away; the proffered salary which would pay for college courses toward her certification as a principal this winter made her stay. Her goal was to get that position by the time she was thirty, three years from now. Through gritted teeth she murmured, "I agree to your terms."

Again she looked directly at him, a warm pink color on her flawless cheeks.

Alexander felt uncomfortable about the trial period. He wanted to rescind it, but caution kept him silent. He didn't know if she could write. If she had to be let go at the end of the month's probation, an experienced writer would still be able to do it. No, better let her prove herself.

Making a quick decision, he said, "This will be your office." His original plan had the writer working in the mansion library, but in this office, he could keep tabs on her easily.

Brenda looked around the small room. Definitely,

6 *Ludima Gus Burton*

the power of space was not to be hers. The only advantage of this office was its proximity to the cars.

"Since I have to order a computer and printer, you can't start work on the book today," he said. "Please be here at nine tomorrow."

With this clear dismissal, Brenda nodded her head and walked out of the office. Her back was stiff under her coat and her head held as high as a queen's. She wasn't slinking out of His Majesty's sight like a whipped dog.

Alexander admired her spirit. He noticed that a few hairpins had escaped from Brenda's bun at the nape of her slender neck.

If he plucked out the remaining pins, would her hair cascade like a tempting waterfall?

Thrusting the thought away, he reached for the phone to order the office equipment.

Brenda's thoughts rode a roller coaster on her return to her apartment in Canfield. One moment, she rushed headlong into the depths of depression. Her summer job could be gone. Financially, this would play havoc with her plans for the money earned. Oh, well, she'd find something else. She'd worked in fast-food places before for extra money.

Then anger rocked her. How dare Alexander Stone, the world-famous playboy, look down on her and belittle her? Since when had he become an authority on the craft of writing?

Brenda hit the steering wheel in frustration. Why,

The Tycoon and the Schoolteacher 7

oh why, hadn't she immediately told him about the four short stories that had been published? That she had finished the first draft on her novel?

All because he couldn't have been more handsome in life than the pictures she had seen of him. That was what had addled her brains and made her appear so incompetent. Even in his jeans he looked magnificent.

The book must mean more to him than she had realized. Whoops! Hadn't she said "this little book?" That's why he had turned to stone. Funny how he reverted in his expressions and actions to the qualities of his last name.

She had a theory that a person tended to reflect his name. She certainly acted like a Brenda—practical, dull, and ordinary. Someone had once told her that she should have a Spanish name to go with her black hair and her olive skin. Would she act differently if her name had been Lolita?

Tomorrow she'd be a Brenda and again wear her black suit. Businesslike, with a firm control over her personal feelings.

She gave a sniff. Why was she wasting a moment on how she looked or how to act? Alexander Stone wouldn't even notice. The notorious race-car driver and most sought-after bachelor would hardly make a pass at her.

In high school, even Aunt Margaret's love hadn't been enough to erase the damage of being called a beanpole. In the classroom, however, with her exuberant students, she felt at home. With them she could smile and laugh and enjoy life.

Then Philip Webster had come to teach Physics in her high school. To her delight and wonder, he had asked her for a date. Before long, she gave him her heart. She ignored her inner disquiet when he often acted dictatorial. It was magical that a man as darkly handsome and as brilliant as Philip was content to be with her.

She had refrained from asking him to drive more slowly, though her heart was in her mouth at his excessive speed. If only, if only, she had. He might still be alive today and her heart not broken. The tears of grief welled up in her eyes, making it difficult for her to see the road. She brushed them away. The man she had loved was gone and no amount of recriminations would bring him back.

It was ironic that she would be writing her first book about cars. She had struggled about the topic of the book and had delayed giving her answer to Charles Stone. She didn't want to write about cars and be reminded daily of how Philip had died. However, the salary was too good to refuse. And she hoped she had made her peace with the past.

Since she was free for the rest of the day, she would spend the time getting more familiar with the pictures of the cars in the family collection Charles Stone had given her. She wondered again why he had chuckled when he wished her luck. Had he known he was throwing her into the den of a wolf? At any rate, it

The Tycoon and the Schoolteacher 9

was too bad his nephew hadn't inherited his uncle's kindness and warmth.

After Brenda left, Alexander's conscience flayed him. He hadn't been fair with her. He should have hired his own writer and not asked his uncle to do it for him. He was sure he'd never have chosen her.

But he'd give Brenda Harrison a month to prove herself. After all, she had made a favorable impression upon his wily uncle. Feeling uneasy, he remembered his uncle's chuckle when he informed him his writer would be appearing today on his doorstep.

It was logical for her to have the small office. Brenda would be close to the cars and the garage where he worked on his new sport designs. He could keep close tabs on her—her writing, that is.

By the close of day, Alexander smiled with satisfaction at the transformation of the office. He hoped the change would please Miss Brenda Harrison. He didn't want to admit that her opinion was important. After all, she could be gone after a month. Then he remembered the determined look she had given him before she walked away. It had been the look of a fighter accepting his challenge. Miss Harrison was no quitter.

He wondered why this thought made him feel good enough to whistle as he returned to the gear shift problem in his car.

*   *   *

10   *Ludima Gus Burton*

The next morning, Alexander waited for Brenda's arrival.

It was heralded by the clunking noises that grated on his automotive sensibilities, as much today as they did yesterday. No car should sound so out of tune with its various parts. His ear was accustomed to the powerful purring of his sports cars.

Not only did the car sound terrible, it needed a paint job as well. Brenda should buy a new car . . .

Alexander shifted his feet. It was easy for him to say this. Money had never been a problem for him. It might not be the case for Brenda. And he had put her on a month's probationary period.

He felt like a cad. But the book was important to him. He couldn't let pity sabotage his plans. If she didn't work out as a writer, he'd find her a job somewhere in his company. Alexander felt a little better with that magnanimous decision.

As yesterday, she was in the black suit. Did she think that pulling her hair back so severely and hiding her expressive blue eyes behind glasses made her unattractive to him?

Why did she dress this way?

Alexander stood in the shadows as Brenda hurried into the office. Her gasp of approval pleased him.

In the refurbished office, the old articles had been replaced by a computer center, a soft green rug, a small armchair, and a side table holding a coffeemaker.

"Does this suit you?" Alexander asked. He came up

The Tycoon and the Schoolteacher 11

close behind her. A tantalizing fragrance from her hair drifted to him and made his heart flutter.

"Oh, yes! Thank you."

Her smile captivated him. He had never seen a beautiful face so transformed to greater loveliness by a mere smile. Mere? Hardly. It came from within and entered her eyes to make them sparkle. And Alexander felt that from this moment on, his life would be different because this petite, intriguing woman had put her smiling stamp on him.

"Thank you," she said again.

Her quiet words and the look which went with them pleased Alexander out of all proportion. He wanted to do more than redecorate a room for her. The women he knew desired his money and social position. Brenda brought out unexpected emotions. Why, in such a short time, did she make him think of her as more than a faceless employee?

To hide his disturbing feelings, he answered, with a negligible shrug of his shoulders. "It's nothing."

A pained, hurt look appeared in Brenda's eyes, replacing the pleasure that had been there a minute before. The smile disappeared also.

"I'll do my best on this book," she said and sat down at the computer with her back to him.

Alexander was nonplussed. Women lingered in his presence; they didn't turn their backs to him, no matter what he said or did. If this was her way to capture his attention, she was doing a good job of it. However, he had the unhappy feeling she wasn't doing that.

"When can I expect to see a sample of your work?" he asked, deliberately taunting her for turning her back on him.

Brenda slowly swiveled her chair to face him. She had taken off her glasses and directed the full force of her stormy gaze at him. Temper caused two red spots on her white cheeks.

Alexander saw by her pursed lips the effort she exerted to keep control of her feelings. His request was calculated to make her angry, but he didn't expect to see how beautiful her flash of temper made her.

"This is Tuesday." Her voice was pitched so low that Alexander had to bend down to hear her. Again her fragrance made his heart beat faster. "By Friday, I'll show you an outline and a draft of my introduction. More than that, I can't promise you because I need to look at the cars in the garage—"

"It's a showroom," he corrected her.

"... and get acquainted with its contents," Brenda finished without giving him further satisfaction of how he irritated her. If Alexander proved to be difficult to please, it wouldn't be a pleasant summer job after all. No matter, she was in the middle of a beautiful setting, with acres of velvet lawns and patterned flower gardens with their riot of blooms. She'd look at them and forget Alexander's frowns.

"Friday will be fine. Don't worry if it takes a few days longer."

"I assure you, Mr. Stone, a deadline doesn't worry me."

The Tycoon and the Schoolteacher 13

Brenda lifted her chin—and tried to ignore the hairpin that slipped out of her hair and landed at his feet. Her hair was too thick and straight to be imprisoned in a smooth bun. Tomorrow, she'd braid it tightly.

When Alexander didn't reach down to pick up the hairpin, she relaxed; he hadn't noticed it. She felt he was watching her every move. His attention unnerved her. Was she so different from the women in his life? After all, she was on a job, dressed accordingly, and behaved in a businesslike manner.

Not knowing what else to say or do, Brenda swung her chair back to the computer and began typing.

Alexander saw she had turned her back on him—again!

He looked at the bun and saw that several more hairpins were ready to fall out. He muffled a chuckle to see that Brenda's hair wanted to be free from its bonds. Was it indicative of her inner spirit? He hoped he would be around the day her spirit broke free from its bonds.

Chapter Two

After Alexander left, Brenda slumped in her chair. At last her heart began to slow down and she took deep breaths to fill her oxygen-starved lungs.

The book was the only reason she was going to see him at all. After she submitted some fabulous pages and he had confidence in her writing ability, he'd leave her alone.

His corporate office was in the Canfield Towers. The showroom for the high-priced luxury cars, both domestic and foreign, was on the ground floor. Surely, he would be there all the time either selling the cars or at his desk ordering them.

But he had said he was working on a car here, both yesterday and today. His grease-spotted jeans attested to it. Was it one of his new car designs? She remem-

The Tycoon and the Schoolteacher   15

bered reading a short article about him entering a competition on them.

Was it a secret project? Would she be barred from the garage? Not that she could ever be guilty of being an industrial spy since she knew nothing about what was under the hood of a car. She'd never be able to give away any secrets about an engine. If only her old, faithful Chevy, her means of transportation to this job in the country, would last the summer.

Brenda looked at the clock. She had time to go into the garage—no, showroom!—and start getting acquainted with the collection first hand. She now knew they were being housed in three large buildings. This one had the oldest cars, dating from 1886 to 1915.

She took a deep breath and entered the showroom.

It was so large. She felt like an ant. Towering green plants were beautifully situated to separate the cars.

Each car was showcased on a carpeted platform, with indirect lighting glistening on the paint and chrome. They had been painstakingly restored to mint condition.

For the next few hours, she took pages of notes and fell in love with the cars. She was going to give her everything to preserve on paper what only her eyes could actually see. She wanted to be able to share with others what only "the rich and the famous," by invitation, had seen. How pleased Alexander's parents would be with his unusual gift.

On the way to work this morning, she had tentatively decided she'd present the cars in the order they were in the showroom. How could she make them come alive? A person reading the book should feel as if he was actually on the floor of the showroom, letting imagination transport him to this beautiful estate.

At noon, Brenda stopped to eat and reached for the brown-bag lunch she had prudently brought. As she munched on her ham-and-cheese sandwich, she wished she had asked Alexander some practical questions about her work schedule.

As though her wish gave birth to the deed, Alexander showed up at the office door. He watched her put the last bite of her sandwich in her mouth.

"I apologize. I should have made arrangements for your lunch to be brought in."

"It's all right." Brenda swallowed her food and tried not to choke on it. "I prefer to bring my lunch and eat whenever I find time."

Although Alexander admired her independence, he felt an unreasonable dissatisfaction with it. Most women tried to inveigle a luncheon invitation from him.

"I have some questions," she said. "Your uncle suggested I work from nine to five o'clock, five days a week until September first. Is this okay with you?"

"I don't think we need to be so structured. As far as I'm concerned, you can flex your hours."

"I'll keep regular hours and even work on the weekends, if necessary," she said. "This book has an August deadline and I'll meet it."

"Suit yourself. I'll let my uncle's office handle your

The Tycoon and the Schoolteacher 17

salary and whatever withholding there is. You'll get your weekly check on Friday afternoon before you leave. My involvement will be supervising the writing of this book."

He strode to the door. "I'll be seeing you."

Brenda was relieved to know his uncle would be handling the financial details. Alexander might have questioned the amount of her salary. It was going to be harrowing to have Alexander looking over her shoulder while she worked on the book.

How cruel fate had been to play this trick on her. She had thought Charles Stone would be her employer, not his nephew.

She wondered if he understood how difficult it was to create a book. Albeit this was a nonfiction book with illustrations and narrative and no dialogue; still, the words had to get on paper and be interesting to the reader.

It was to be a private publication. How many copies? Certainly a limited edition—another evidence of the immense wealth in the Stone family.

Brenda went back into the showroom for the rest of the afternoon to take notes.

She was on her knees before a 1905 Buick, Model C, trying to read the fine print about the engine on the plaque. She had removed her jacket and unbuttoned the top of her blouse. Her narrow skirt had been hiked up to allow her to kneel.

When Alexander walked into the showroom, he admired the expanse of her legs.

18   *Ludima Gus Burton*

"It's after six o'clock. Why haven't you gone home?" Alexander's brusque question behind her startled Brenda.

Trying to get up in a hurry, she hit her head with a resounding whack on the fender of the old car.

"Ouch!"

Chapter Three

Brenda rubbed the top of her head.

Alexander helped her to her feet.

"How badly are you hurt?"

"It's nothing. I feel so foolish."

"Let me see."

Very gently, Alexander's fingers tunneled under her hair over her scalp. The action loosened the pins holding the bun at the nape of her neck. Her soft, shiny black hair fell in a wavy waterfall down her back.

Alexander's fingers stilled their search.

The beauty of her hair awed him. He wanted to bury his face in its fragrance. He forced himself to continue probing her scalp. A lump was forming; the skin, however, wasn't broken.

"You may have a headache—"

"Don't be silly. It was just a bump." She grabbed her hair and began to braid it. "This hair—I should cut it short."

"No! Don't ever do that!"

Brenda's surprise at his reaction to her casual remark showed in her gaze. She didn't answer his command but went to work subduing her hair. While he watched, her fingers seized the hair and divided it into three strands. She wondered if he had ever seen a woman braid her hair. Probably not, if his stare was any indication.

Finished, she hunted in her pocket for a rubber band with which to secure the ends. She tossed the heavy braid over her shoulder. Soft, short, wisps of hair framed her face. Gone was the austere look of a schoolteacher.

She dropped the hairpins he'd picked up into her pocket.

"Why are you still here?" he asked.

"I forgot the time. The cars fascinated me."

She pointed to the car whose fender had connected with her head. "Look at the red cushioned seats and the wooden yellow spokes on this 1905 Buick. I had no idea they liked bright colors back then." She frowned and said thoughtfully, "Don't think I need to include the technical stuff about it having a two-cylinder horizontal end reversal gearbox—all Greek to me!"

"It would be to my mother, too," Alexander agreed. "Do what you think best."

The Tycoon and the Schoolteacher   21

Doubts of his gift assailed Alexander.

"Perhaps this book isn't such a good idea, after all," he said thoughtfully.

"Oh, no!" Brenda cried, laying her hand on his arm. "It's a wonderful idea. This collection needs to be preserved in a book. What if you had a fire and all the cars burned?"

Alexander looked into Brenda's eyes and saw her sincere concern. He liked the feel of her warm fingers on him. Put like that, the book made sense.

Alexander followed Brenda to the office and leaned against the door. After she covered the keyboard and picked up her suit jacket, he clicked off the light and followed her to her car.

He unnerved Brenda with his silence, his eyes hooded. What was he thinking? She never should have touched his arm, but she was so accustomed to encouraging her students with her light touches. Alexander, however, held himself aloof. She had to remember who and what he was.

Still silent, he opened the door. He grimaced at the screech. Brenda gave a sympathetic smile.

"Good night," she said and put on her seat belt.

"Good night. Drive carefully." He hated to see her drive away in such an unsafe piece of junk.

Brenda felt his intent gaze follow her departure. And wished, unwisely, there would be a Cinderella ending to this summer.

Alexander stayed where he was long after he no longer could see or hear her car.

22   *Ludima Gus Burton*

Her touch had been warm.

Alexander drew in his breath with a startled hiss. He mustn't be affected by it. Whatever was he thinking? He didn't need or want any personal involvement with his writer.

Still, she stayed in his thoughts for the rest of the evening.

"Good morning. How's the head?"

At Alexander's cheerful greeting and question, Brenda smiled at him. He again wore his jeans. Though she chided herself, a happy feeling spread through her because he was going to be nearby today.

"Fine. It was only a little bump on a very hard head."

"Before you get started, would you like a tour of our compound?" Alexander asked.

"I'd love it. I haven't been to the other showrooms." Brenda saw Alexander's gaze fall to the sensible flat-heeled oxfords on her slender feet. With her plain white blouse and narrow black skirt, she must look like the schoolteacher she was. Well, she wasn't glamorous and she wasn't trying to attract Alexander's attention.

Alexander matched his long stride to her shorter one and Brenda walked sedately beside him. He took her first to see the other two buildings containing the rest of the collection. She had made only a small dent in writing about the cars in the first building. She almost threw up her hands in despair.

The Tycoon and the Schoolteacher   23

Alexander saw her worried frown.

"What's the matter?"

"I've so much to do. I should get back."

Alexander took firm hold of her arm. "You can see the rest of the compound without endangering the completion of the book."

Apparently, the garage wasn't off limits to her. The latest sports car he was working on interested her. She loved the light blue color.

The four luxury cars in a converted carriage house made Brenda hide a smile. Honestly, she should park her car behind all the buildings. It was completely out of place.

Walking slowly back to the office, Brenda looked between the two showrooms onto the green fields behind them.

"Am I seeing what I think I am?" she asked.

Alexander grinned. "Yes, it's a racetrack."

The size of the Stone estate impressed her anew. She thought of her small studio apartment which would probably fit into the butler's pantry in the mansion!

"I test run my cars on it," Alexander explained. His voice held a tinge of longing. "Doesn't compare to my racing days, but better than nothing."

"You men!" Brenda's voice was full of scorn. "All you think about is how fast your cars will go. Even back in 1905, the Automotive Association was formed primarily to warn motorists of police traps!"

Ignoring the surprise in Alexander's gaze, she left

him standing there, speechless, at her unwarranted attack.

He chuckled out loud. Brenda didn't hesitate to speak her views.

What was her hang-up about speed? Something in her past?

He shrugged his shoulders. His Sports Car XL should be ready to be tested as soon as he went back to the garage.

Gradually, Brenda simmered down. She never should have turned on Alexander. He had every right to do what he wanted with his life—even throw it away—as Philip had done.

She, along with the rest of the world, had watched on TV when Alexander crashed his car during the Grand Prix. It was a miracle he sustained only bruises and a broken collarbone. Some sense must have been knocked into him, because he announced a week later that he was leaving professional racing for good. Not, however, from testing his cars on his own private racetrack.

Men and their cars. From her research, she learned the inventors were obsessed with speed—making each improvement with that thought in mind. Even back in 1916, a limousine—a Rolls-Royce—could exceed 65 miles per hour! She could imagine the surprise, fear, and outrage of a horse-and-buggy culture to see the noisy mechanical monsters hurtling down a quiet country road.

The Tycoon and the Schoolteacher   25

Just as these quiet acres of beauty would be violated by the roar of Alexander's car. Well, not a roar, but a powerful purring of a well-oiled engine as it accelerated to its top speed. She had to admit, her car heralded its coming with noises no respectable mechanic would tolerate.

Brenda gave a full, unrestrained laugh at the thought. It didn't embarrass her one bit, either.

Remembering she had to show Alexander some pages of her book on Friday, Brenda made herself comfortable. Her fingers flew on the keys of her computer. She had to remember to tell Alexander to write his dedication.

Her fingers stopped typing. Her thoughts left the office. She saw herself being introduced to his parents as the writer of the book, in front of all their guests. She'd be wearing a fabulous sequined gown with her hair in an elaborate style to make her look beautiful and regal. Alexander would be looking down onto her face, his gaze filled with pride—and yes—even more—

The sudden roar of a car engine shattered Brenda's daydream. She quickly ran outside and raced to the top of the hill overlooking the racetrack.

The car was the blue one she had seen in the garage. At least it was the only car on the track, with no danger of a rival car running into it.

She heard the car come around a curve. The streak of blue went around and around at a reasonable speed. Philip had tried to explain, with male logic, why a car had to be able to go 125 miles an hour when much lower speed limits were posted on every highway. She hadn't accepted his explanation. If only he had listened to her pleadings.

She breathed a sigh of relief. Evidently, this was going to be a normal road test as one would take on a public highway. Alexander stepped on the brakes. The car stopped as though on a dime. Then Alexander started up the car slowly.

Relieved, Brenda turned to go back.

She heard the burst of speed as Alexander accelerated the car from zero to sudden great speed. She was in time to see the car shoot like a bullet around a curve and out of sight on the part of the track hidden from her view by trees.

A screech of brakes and the sound of a car hitting an obstacle had Brenda running down the hill.

She reached the scene before the four mechanics. Alexander was already pulling himself free from the air bag and seat belt. He was swearing words Brenda had never heard before. The relief of seeing he wasn't hurt turned Brenda's fear to anger.

"You fool, you foolish jerk! Why didn't you drive slower? You could have killed yourself—" She stopped when she heard the muffled chuckles coming from the mechanics and saw the thunderous cloud descend on Alexander's face.

"Back off, Miss Brenda Harrison. I'm not one of your students. This is my car and I'll do what I please with it." Brenda's criticism of his driving skills in

The Tycoon and the Schoolteacher   27

front of his men irritated him. He couldn't understand her emotional outburst. He wasn't hurt and the car was fine. True, that little tree would never be the same.

"For your information, it wasn't me or the car. It was a patch of wet mud that caused a slide off the track. No big deal."

Feeling her face flush a beet-red, Brenda felt she was the fool. He was right. She was wrong to scold him as she did her students.

She turned and ran up the hill.

Her hands were trembling so much she had difficulty opening the door to the office. For a few minutes, it was like reliving the news about Philip's accident. She wondered if she was ever going to get over it.

Alexander's road test had been proceeding so well a few minutes ago. The accident happened in a flash. She had barely turned her back. How quickly life could end and everything be changed.

Alexander had neatly put her in her place. She had acted ridiculous and she felt embarrassed.

She helped herself to water from a carafe.

"Brenda." Alexander had entered quietly. "Look at me."

She turned to face him, forcing herself to look into his eyes.

"I'm sorry I lost my temper." His smile was beguiling. "I can't remember the last time anyone yelled at me." He continued to smile. "Besides, what happened today was no big deal, honestly. At least I know the air bag works."

"I'm sorry I lost control," she answered. She wasn't going to tell him about Philip. She couldn't bear his sympathy. "I tend to treat adults like my kids in school. When my students do something dangerous, I tell them."

Alexander laughed. "You don't need to worry about me. I really do know what I'm doing out on the track."

"I'll try to remember that."

"Will you look at future test runs?"

Brenda shook her head. "No, thanks. You can do it all on your own."

The next morning, Alexander was there to open the door and help her out of the car.

"All is forgiven?" He smiled at her and Brenda smiled back.

Time seemed to stop as she gazed into his gray eyes. Her breath caught in her throat and her heart hammered in her chest. For a world-stopping moment, she thought he was going to kiss her.

With a soft sigh, she stepped back.

To cover her confusion at the depth of her desire for his kiss, she said the first thing to come into her head. "I was glad to see you have air bags."

"It's the law." Normal conversation suited him, too. He had wanted to kiss Brenda's tempting lips. It would have been a mistake in judgment. Much, much too soon—but it heightened the anticipation of that future date . . . for he would kiss her . . .

"Only for new cars. And not in your race cars. You

The Tycoon and the Schoolteacher   29

didn't have one when you crashed at the Grand Prix."
Brenda felt more at ease now. She had defused the
moment of madness.

"You watched the race? I'm surprised."

"I happened to turn on the TV a few minutes before
you crashed. You were fortunate you weren't killed.
Did you decide you had pushed Lady Luck far
enough?"

"Yes, though I had been thinking of it. The crash
was the deciding factor."

"Don't you miss the excitement and the thrills? Ever
want to go back to it?"

"Sometimes, but I get a little of it when I test my
cars." When Brenda's eyes widened, he said quickly,
"I don't take chances. Yesterday was a fluke. I didn't
see the mud puddle. Believe me, I don't take chances."
He couldn't very well tell her that he'd been thinking
of her instead of concentrating on the test.

"Your life is yours to do with as you see fit. I'm
sorry I made a scene yesterday. I won't interfere
again."

Alexander gave a chuckle. "I have a feeling you will
whether I give you my permission or not. The teacher
in you will rise again," he teased.

Brenda felt the blush spreading from her neck to
color her cheeks. She recalled Philip saying, "Don't
order me around, love. I'm not one of your students."
And it was the same with Alexander.

"I'm curious. Do women buy your sports cars?"

30 *Ludima Gus Burton*

"Not as a rule. A very young woman may, just to show off and attract guys."

"So, your advertising is aimed at men?"

"Why the questions? Sounds like you're on a women's liberation crusade." Alexander's eyes narrowed.

Brenda looked right at him. "I think, at times, women would like one of your sports cars instead of a four-door sedan."

Alexander threw out his hands. "Don't do this to me. I'm not going to change my designs to suit a woman. She'd probably want a pink one."

"Don't be insulting. I'd buy one just like the blue one and I'm a woman."

Brenda tossed her head and a few hairpins fell to the floor. With a disgusted cry, she reached back and pushed in the remaining pins. She muttered, "This hair—just won't stay pinned up."

"So let it down. I like it that way."

At his words, Brenda's heart gave a skip, but she said primly, "It's not professional."

"How do you wear it when you teach?"

"As I do here." Brenda continued, "Forget my hairstyle and go back to your cars—"

"Yes?"

"Since I assume you're interested in increasing sales, I'd suggest you make a slight adjustment to the seats for women—"

"Slight adjustment—"

Brenda ignored his sputter and kept on talking. "The

The Tycoon and the Schoolteacher   31

1964 Oldsmobile Starfire convertible was built to appeal to the 'Little Woman.' It had power-everything, a steering wheel which could tilt to seven positions, and a seat in six positions. So there! It can be done!"

"Lady, you don't know what you're talking about and I want you to stop right there." A deep frown furrowed his brow and a high color appeared in his cheeks. Brenda had as much as told him he wasn't as capable as the old car manufacturers. "You stick to what you profess you know, your writing. Maybe I'll make some 'slight' adjustments on it!"

With his threat hanging between them, he left the office, banging the door shut.

Well! He had put her in her place and rightly so. She'd have to keep her suggestions to herself. Alexander had also reminded her that she better have some good pages for him soon.

Alexander seethed and struck the dent on the car harder than he intended. Why did Brenda have to be like other women? Trying to invade his territory? He wanted his sports cars to be designed and equipped for men. Heaven only knew that women were entitled to equal rights, but this was too much. Some areas needed to be sacrosanct for men only, and women should accept that edict.

His sports cars were special. Until today, for men only—with no complaints. But here was Brenda saying so easily "make a slight adjustment to the seat." What, bring up the seat for her beautiful, not as long as a man's, legs to reach the pedals? It would take more than a slight adjustment.

Another thing. Why did she hide her beauty behind her hideous black clothes and glasses? It looked as though she intended to wear them day after day. Did she dress like this when teaching? Did it help her maintain discipline more easily?

A schoolteacher. He couldn't imagine her standing, a mere five-feet-two inches tall, in front of a class full of burly high school thugs. How did she do it? Even if she wore her three-inch heels while teaching, the boys must tower over her.

Another mystery. Did she stand all day in school in those high heels? Perhaps he'd find out some day.

Enough about this matter. It made him feel good that she had been concerned about him yesterday at the crash scene. He chuckled, remembering being called a foolish jerk. And realized it was because she had been afraid for him.

A warm glow came over him. Most of his life he had fought his battles alone, with the admonition to be strong and to show no weakness.

Her concern for his welfare was in contrast to the people in his past who were only interested in the wild chances he took in his race cars. The more risks he took, the more women sought him. They sensed the danger and thrived on it. What a foolish jerk he had been—just as Brenda said.

That life was behind him. The cars he designed were as safe as he could make them. He had no control

The Tycoon and the Schoolteacher   33

over the feelings or wishes or frustrations of the men who drove them.

"Guys, how bad is the damage?" he asked his mechanics.

"Not bad, mostly dents. We'll have it fixed in no time." Bill gave a laugh. "Hope you were able to make your peace with the schoolteacher. Boy, she reminds me of my little old math teacher. Could she cut me down to size—even when she was looking up to me. I'll bet Miss Harrison does the same in her class."

"I ate my humble pie. She said, however, she wasn't going to watch a test run again."

"She'll hear it, though. So you better not crash again. Can't have her worrying over a big lug like you."

Alexander nodded his head. He was used to the easy camaraderie of his men.

As with the men, Brenda's smile worked her magic on him. Her hair, also, was a redeeming asset, but only if it was flowing free. Why she strangled it in that tight bun, he'd never understand.

A laugh boomed forth. Her hair didn't want to be imprisoned any more than he wanted it to be. Look how easily it expelled those silly hairpins!

He sobered. Her beauty or lack of it wasn't a factor. Tomorrow he would be reading her pages. And she might very well be on her way out.

Tomorrow.

Chapter Four

Brenda handed ten typed pages to Alexander.

"You'll find me in the showroom," she said and made her escape into the showroom with more haste than grace.

Alexander watched Brenda's slender figure disappear out of sight. Still wearing black. Ye gads, this wasn't a funeral parlor! He scowled and started to read.

Brenda Harrison knew how to write.

Warm pleasure pulsated through his veins. He didn't have to fire her; she was here until September. He would see her and spar with her every day or until he lost interest in her. He argued with himself that it was only because she was different, very different, from the women in his life. And she ignored him,

34

The Tycoon and the Schoolteacher   35

turned her back on him, frequently walked away from him.

Her appeal would wear off as soon as he had won her. The challenge was in the pursuit. Winning was a letdown. Besides, any kind of a personal relationship with a prim schoolteacher was out of the question. Short-term relationships were for him. Brenda didn't fit in. He'd bet she was an old-fashioned woman who wanted a ring on her finger and a forever-after commitment.

He wasn't ready for commitment this summer. The years were, however, flying by. He should marry and produce an heir before he reached forty. He needed a woman to grace his home, to entertain his business associates and friends, and to be on the committees of family-sponsored charitable organizations. He still had years to look around for a suitable wife.

His rebellious days were behind him. He winced to remember the last ten years when the international racing world embraced him. He had fallen into the maelstrom of adulation, parties and beautiful women, trying to forget his family and responsibilities.

"What's the verdict?" Brenda's voice broke into his thoughts. She had returned quietly and stood before him.

Alexander smiled at her. "You pass. Isn't that what you tell your students?"

Relief flooded Brenda. "Yes, that's right. But I personally would have preferred you to say I got an A-plus."

"Hey, and give you a swelled head? I like what

you've done and your plan for the whole book. But," he frowned, "I don't think this will keep you busy all summer. After all, there are only fifty cars in the collection—fifty pages—a page a day—"

"You're wrong on the page count. For one thing, the photographs will take up several pages besides whatever I write about the car. I'm sure I'll want to give more information for some cars because of their interesting history."

He gave her a mock bow. "I stand corrected. You want me to stand in the corner?" Mischief and good humor danced in his eyes.

"No, only write your dedication to your parents."

All of Alexander's good feeling drained out of him. This simple request brought back all his failures in English composition. This little English teacher was going to mark his work with her red pen. He recalled the disappointed look on his mother's face. They were his only poor marks in his school life.

"You do it," he ordered Brenda.

"No," she answered him right back. "It's your gift. Your dedication in your own words is vital." She frowned at Alexander. "For heaven's sake, I'm not your secretary who has to do all of your writing for you. Why the big deal? A couple of sentences. Anyone can do that."

"Fine. I'll do it," Alexander said in poor grace. "Just because I like your introduction doesn't mean you can slide along."

Though Alexander was immediately sorry he had

The Tycoon and the Schoolteacher 37

lashed out at her, he wasn't going to apologize. He had every right to say what he did. With a brief nod in her direction, he left the office.

Brenda heard the Porsche spin its tires as he drove away. He was in a snit—the only word her brain could come up with. It was all out of proportion. It could be a short dedication. She'd gladly do it for him. But, no, he had to write it. She met with similar opposition from students who had a writing problem.

Brenda tapped her thumbnail against her teeth. Could it be that Alexander had a writing disorder? It was possible. With secretaries and computers, all with their spell-check and grammar-checks at his command, Alexander didn't need to write anything.

She smiled. If she got a very correct print-out sheet, she wouldn't be surprised.

Brenda shoved her pages into the briefcase and covered the computer. She was going home early. She had weathered the storms of the first week. What a contrast the beautiful, peaceful environment around her building was to the turbulent feelings within her and the verbal encounters with her charismatic employer. She needed the weekend to step back and get a true perspective of how she should act this summer.

She swung between a hope Alexander would stay away from her to her desire to talk—even disagree—with him all the time.

Not the proper behavior for an employee. It was so

hard for her to remember she wasn't in her classroom. Definitely, she couldn't order Alexander around.

Buying groceries, doing her laundry, and cleaning the apartment took all her time on Saturday. On Sunday, Brenda made her new curtains.

As she sewed, Brenda realized that sewing by hand freed her mind to think. Already, memories of Simpson Central School and her life there were fading. She was concerned that Philip's face was becoming harder to recall. She had loved him, hadn't she? He had loved her, hadn't he? His mother had hated her and made no effort to hide it.

She herself had overlooked his dictatorial ways because he could also be a very loving man. One weekend they had looked at a small beach cottage Philip said he wanted to buy. He never spoke of it again so that idea must have fallen through.

With a sigh, she picked up her sewing. The past was the past. She had a future. Smiling, she spun a dream about the principal's job she was aiming for. Her experience at an inner-city school like Hilliard High would look good on her résumé.

Monday morning, Brenda enjoyed the beauty of the colorful riot of daffodils and tulips in the many gardens of the estate. The blue sky added to the color of the flowers. What an ideal place to work.

She took a deep breath of the sweet air. She had already met the four gardeners who toiled to make the

The Tycoon and the Schoolteacher 39

gardens beautiful. How much joy the wealthy, because they had the money to pay for labor, missed in not doing it themselves. She wondered if Alexander ever got down on his knees to help a flower grow.

Alexander's car wasn't in his parking space. She wouldn't see him today. Why was she still wearing black? Why had she even worn her high heels today? Surely, now she could relax her self-imposed dress code. Still, she enjoyed seeing Alexander's reaction. And hear his pointed hints about liking color, especially red. She had ignored him and continued her charade.

She could easily imagine Alexander in a business suit, tailored to perfection. He would take on his Stone persona—cold, unsmiling, and arrogant. A person's name did affect behavior. No way could Alexander escape his family name! He was always called by his full name. Only his housekeeper called him Alex.

Brenda picked up her photographs and entered the showroom. Idle speculation wasted time. As it was, she was taking her pages home each night to revise.

Alexander coasted to a quiet stop in front of the showroom. Three days had passed since he last saw Brenda. He wanted to be with her, to see if what he had been imagining would come true—that her blue eyes would light up with joy and her smile would shine brightly.

She wasn't in the office.

He took off his maroon tie and unbuttoned the top of his shirt. His jacket fell on the chair.

The door to the showroom was open and he entered quietly.

A pair of black pumps lay where they had been kicked off. That answered his question about how torturous they were to wear. Why hadn't she worn her sensible oxfords today?

Silently, Alexander proceeded down the line of cars.

The inevitible suit coat was folded neatly on the hood of a 1907 Ford. Alexander smiled and walked further.

A trail of hairpins pointed the way. Alexander almost laughed out loud. What was coming next? His heart thumped in his chest.

At the end of the showroom, Brenda was sitting cross-legged on the floor. Her white blouse was unbuttoned. The full black skirt bunched above her knees, giving a charming view of her ankles. Her lustrous hair fell in a concealing wave over half of her face. Humming a country-western tune, she chewed on the end of a pencil until she made a notation on her pad. Photographs of the cars were spread in a semicircle before her.

Wishing he had a camera, Alexander gazed on her. This was Brenda in a natural pose. The dull suits and pinned-up hair had been a cover-up.

Becoming conscious of someone's scrutiny, Brenda looked up. The pencil fell to the floor and her hand covered her mouth as she uttered a surprised, "Oh!"

The Tycoon and the Schoolteacher   41

She attempted to stand. The folds of her skirt hindered her. If Alexander's hand hadn't grasped hers firmly, she would have fallen backwards. He pulled her up, bringing her against him.

She clutched his shirt. His heart pounded under her hand. Her head tilted back and she gazed into the warm gray eyes of the man she had missed seeing for three days. An eternity passed before she gave a sigh and stepped away from him. She had thought, for one fleeting moment, that he was going to kiss her.

Alexander was angry at himself for not kissing her. Her lips had been so close and the look in her eyes had beckoned him. Not knowing how she would react, he had hesitated too long.

"Comfortable?" He smiled down at her.

Knowing he had seen her discarded attire down the line of cars, Brenda nodded. "You caught me in the act. Those shoes are not for walking."

She knelt down to pick up the photographs. Alexander helped her.

Brenda tried to ignore her rapidly beating heart. She wasn't going to get involved with this playboy. With no effort on his part, his magnetic charm drew her to him. She wished she was able to be light-hearted and at ease with men. Only Philip had been able to make her happy and carefree. Besides, she didn't want to endanger her heart.

"How's the book coming?" Alexander handed her the pictures.

She made sure her fingers didn't touch his.

"I'm pleased with it so far."

Alexander looked down into her animated face. Brenda's enthusiasm and excitement spread to him. More and more, he was glad he had decided on this anniversary gift.

Brenda smiled at him and the dimple in her cheek enchanted him. He had the reckless urge to kiss it. She made him feel like a teenager.

When they had reached her coat, she picked it up. She failed to pick up the hairpins. They made a trail like the bread crumbs dropped by the children in the fairy tale. Perhaps they were the only ones she possessed and her hair would hang free. It was a captivating prospect. He looked forward to running his fingers through its luxurious tresses.

He put brakes on his runaway thoughts.

He held her steady so she could slip into her shoes.

"Why do you wear these instruments of torture?" he asked.

"I've gotten used to them. In the classroom I like to have a little bit of an advantage over my tall students. They make them big and tall these days!"

"Aren't you afraid of them?" She should never have spoken about the size of her students. Now he would worry about her.

Brenda shook her head. "I was concerned my first year of teaching, but I learned to stare them down." She gave a giggle. "And I made sure they were sitting

The Tycoon and the Schoolteacher   43

at their desks so I could tower over them when I bawled them out!"

"What was your worst experience?"

"I'll tell you my funniest, instead."

Chapter Five

Brenda leaned against the hood of the yellow 1902 Mercedes, a pleasing background for the blue-black hair Alexander loved to look at. He thought she'd make a striking model.

"My first principal sternly instructed the new teachers not to strike a student. However, we could give them a good shaking." Brenda chuckled. "I had a farm kid named Ezra Hammond. I don't remember now what he was doing—probably talking and making noise—but I went tearing up the aisle. I told him to stand up and I grabbed him by the shoulders to shake him. I had forgotten that he was a foot taller than me and built like a solid tree. When everyone in the class began to laugh, I realized that the only person who was shaking was me, with Ezra not moving an inch."

44

The Tycoon and the Schoolteacher   45

"What did you do?"

"I laughed with them. It was really funny. Believe me, he was the first and last student I tried to shake as a punishment."

"Yes, but what did you do about punishing Ezra?" Alexander didn't find it so funny. Discipline should be enforced and that big lug should pay, as was the case in his military school.

"When we all got through laughing, Ezra apologized," Brenda explained. "After that, he was a model student for me and became my enforcer. I had a time setting him straight—no beating up on others."

Alexander shook his head. He didn't understand how she had survived five years with such lax discipline.

"I've done enough for one day," Brenda said. "As soon as I write twenty-five pages of the first draft, I'll show them to you. All right?"

"Fine. But don't kill yourself."

He looked forward to seeing her, never mind if she was writing or not. Why was he so drawn to her after only a week's acquaintance?

After she put the office in order, he walked with her to the car.

He frowned at the car. It insulted his sensibilities.

Brenda saw his look and hid her amusement. In spite of its dented body and noisy engine, the car took her back and forth to work. In fact, she enjoyed her noisy rides in it. She was going to miss it when it

46 *Ludima Gus Burton*

finally had to go to a junk yard. "My poor car doesn't
belong here at all. I apologize."

"Let me give you a company car—"

"No, thank you. I don't want to be responsible for
your property."

With a wave of her hand and a smile, Brenda noisily
roared away.

Out of range of her hearing, Alexander groaned and
cringed freely. The car belonged in the dump, but
there was nothing he could do about it.

Each day, Brenda worked to limit the facts to be
included in the book. The beautiful robin's-egg blue
Ford Model T, 1909, surprised her. She had only seen
black ones and thought the color was wrong. It wasn't.
That's when she began to appreciate the rare cars in
the Stone collection.

Alexander's grandfather had been wise to rescue the
old cars from extinction. To think, she was the one
who would capture history and make it live outside
this showroom. Alexander deserved the credit for this.

Brenda's battered car made ominous noises it hadn't
before, but it continued to make the trip.

The mechanics began to take bets on how long it
would run. Alexander joined them. The vehicle was
the bane of his mechanical temperament.

Brenda arrived sharply at 9:00 each morning and
left at 5:00.

She didn't understand having the freedom to make

The Tycoon and the Schoolteacher   47

one's own hours as Alexander evidently did. To spend his hours tinkering with a car. For heaven's sake, what could be wrong with a brand-new car, anyway? Yet, there was Alexander, with his four mechanics, under or over or whatever, every time she wandered into the garage during the end of her lunch.

She forced herself to take an hour because she needed to get away from the computer. Some days her eyes got more tired than others and she dreaded the headaches that resulted from the strain.

She gave a rueful smile. She had worn the dark-rimmed glasses only as a prop; unfortunately, she realized she could do with a real pair. She was no competition for the women in Alexander's glamorous life. They probably wore contacts, even changed the color of their eyes. Personally, she wouldn't have contacts for she was too chicken to put the things in her eyes. In the fall, she'd end the charade and get the real thing, what with all those papers to correct.

At 3:00 that day, Brenda turned at the timid knock on her office door.

"Come in, please."

The plump and pleasant-looking woman who entered wore a black dress with a gold antique pin at the neck of the white collar. Her gray hair was in an untidy bun. She smiled broadly at Brenda.

"I'm Mrs. McAllister, Alexander's housekeeper. I've been taking care of my daughter-in-law in Eldon since the day you first arrived. I've come to make you welcome." Her bright blue eyes were kind and motherly. Brenda liked her on the spot.

"Come in and sit down. Would you like a cup of tea? I can make it in a jiffy."

"That would be nice. Ah, Earl Grey tea. Are you English?"

"My Aunt Margaret was and we had tea when we were home at the same time." Brenda smiled at her visitor. She had the feeling she was being observed closely by the housekeeper.

Mrs. McAllister slowly sipped her tea and quietly questioned Brenda about her life. She did it in such a kind manner that Brenda couldn't take offense at her gentle interrogation. She didn't, however, tell her about Philip.

With a little encouragement the housekeeper began to talk about Alexander's childhood. "Alex was a real boy growing up, getting into all kinds of mischief. But he never hurt anyone. He was always laughing and smiling. A real joy to his loving parents. They sure missed him when he went away to school."

"You call him Alex, not Alexander."

"Yes, I'm the only one."

After checking on the time, Mrs. McAllister stood up. "It's time I got back to the house." She heaved herself out of the armchair. "You must come up to see me and meet the others. We should get to know each other. After all, we all want to make Alex happy and comfortable." She gave a deep sigh. "The poor lad shouldn't be living alone in that big house."

The Tycoon and the Schoolteacher   49

"Do you want me to drive you back to the house? It's quite an uphill walk and the sun is hot."

"That would be nice. I get breathless sometimes."

She followed Brenda outside. When Brenda led her to the car, her mouth dropped open.

"This old car is yours? What's the matter with Alex? He should give you one of his cars. He has so many of them."

Brenda quickly explained, "He offered to give me a company car the other day, but I refused." She soothed Mrs. McAllister, "I'm perfectly content with this car. I hope you'll still accept my offer to drive you to the house."

"Of course, my dear." She settled her ample person in the front seat. When Brenda saw the housekeeper's pained expression at the noisy start of engine, she hid her smile. And clearly heard the great sigh of relief on their arrival at the house.

"Thank you. I had my doubts you would get me here in one piece."

Grinning, Brenda waved and drove back to the showroom, trailing a black cloud of exhaust behind her.

In the office, she looked at the calendar. Goodness. The Fourth of July celebration in Canfield was on Saturday. She leaned back in her chair and contemplated. His housekeeper had to be wrong. Alexander couldn't be lonely. He had to have an active social life. Still, why not invite him to take part with her in his city's celebration? It would be a novelty and he just might accept. Though she thought it wise to avoid any personal relationship with her employer, she did want to see him happy.

It didn't have to be construed as anything other than a friendly gesture. It was only for one day, for heaven's sake.

Yes, she'd ask him.

Chapter Six

On Wednesday morning, Brenda debated whether to ask Alexander to join her on Saturday. Should she make her world collide with his at the celebration of the nation's freedom?

She threw her heavy braid over her shoulder. She had come to work with the braid wound around her head, anchored in place by her new supply of hairpins. Enjoying the rush of the wind against her face, she rolled down the window. By the time she reached the Estate, the pins started to fall. Her thick, straight hair again refused the imprisonment.

No more black outfits. Today she wore a trim pair of beige slacks, a short-sleeved pink blouse, and a pair of soft-leather moccasins that made walking comfortable.

52 *Ludima Gus Burton*

Alexander hadn't come to see her yesterday. When he came in today, would he comment on her attire? She could never anticipate his words.

Every day was a new experience. Would this be the way it was in a happy marriage? Never getting bored with each other—feeling a new and exciting emotion just in seeing each other? Thrilled to be together again for another day?

"Hello."

Brenda looked up to see Alexander leaning against the side of the door. He was smiling. Her heart gave a dangerous flip before settling down to normal. He was dressed in slacks and a yellow sports shirt. His suntan took a deeper tone against the yellow. He was the Prince Charming of her daydream.

"Hello, yourself. Has your uncle been keeping you busy?"

"A complication in our sales division needed my attention." He wanted to ask her if she had missed him, but he didn't have the nerve. Why should she? But it would be nice to be missed by her.

Brenda saw his gaze sweep over her.

"I like the outfit. Why did you wear so much black?"

Brenda looked away. She couldn't tell him the real reason. That she knew she could never compare to the glamorous women in his life.

"I thought I should dress like a professional."

"Glad you decided to loosen up." Alexander wanted to say how attractive he found her, no matter what she

The Tycoon and the Schoolteacher   53

wore. He didn't think she would take his words kindly. He also didn't want her to feel he was hitting on her. There was so much in the news about sexual harassment that he was concerned about overstepping the bounds. He wanted Brenda to work here all summer.

"How quickly the time is passing. We'll be celebrating the Fourth of July this coming weekend. What do you do?"

"The Adams have a big barbecue and a swimming pool party. Sometimes I go. Haven't made up my mind this year."

Brenda cocked her head to the side. "The city of Canfield has planned many activities for the weekend. Have you thought of going?"

"No." Alexander turned away. "I'll be in the garage for the rest of the week. The new car needs some kinks ironed out."

"I still don't understand . . ." Brenda let her words trail off.

"What?"

Brenda took a deep breath. "You and your engineers drew all those complicated blueprints and do all kinds of things with them on the computer. When you're finished, the car should be perfect. And still you tinker and tinker."

"Tinker! I don't tinker. I'm an engineer."

Brenda could see she had insulted Alexander. She was sorry, but it didn't make sense to her. She guessed it was one of those "man things" which would always mystify her.

54 *Ludima Gus Burton*

"I'm sorry. I guess I'll never understand. So, go ahead, and don't worry about me. I don't mind leaving those complicated mechanical things to you men to play with."

"Play with!" Now Alexander sounded really upset.

Brenda clapped her hand over her mouth and mumbled, "I'm not saying another word. Forgive me."

Alexander glared at her for a long moment with no forgiveness in his gaze. He shrugged his shoulders.

"I'll see you at lunch. Mrs. Mac is sending us a tray of food at twelve-thirty."

When she was sure Alexander was out of earshot, Brenda's laughter bubbled up and burst out. She had used all the wrong words with Alexander. She was going to have to read up on auto mechanics. She felt it would still be a "man thing" in the end. But, then, Alexander probably thought some of her actions and words were a "woman thing" and just as impossible for him to understand. Oh, well, it all made life interesting.

The lunch was fit for royalty.

"You made a favorable impression on Mrs. Mac," Alexander remarked. "She wanted to meet you right from the start. She checks out my friends. This lunch proves you've passed her test."

"I'm glad. I liked her. I assume she's been with you since you were a little boy."

"Yes, as well as the rest of the staff in the house. My parents are good employers and elicit loyalty."

The Tycoon and the Schoolteacher   55

"She calls you Alex."

Alexander gave a rueful laugh. "She's the only one."

Brenda's eyebrows went up. "You're always called Alexander?"

"Yes. My mother didn't like nicknames."

"I think I'll call you Alex."

"No." The tone was emphatic.

"I'll obey your wish," she said with a grin. She sat down before her computer, ignoring the slamming of the door by her employer on his way out of her office. He didn't need to act so. Of course it wasn't her place as an employee to be so informal with her boss. That's what he meant to convey, evidently.

She wouldn't ask him to come on Saturday.

On Thursday, before she had a chance to think about it, the words spilled out.

"Please go to the Fourth of July parade and picnic with me on Saturday," she said—her boldness was as great a shock to herself as it was to him.

Alexander blinked his eyes and his left eyebrow raised to a V. Could his reticent English teacher be asking him for a date? It was so incomprehensible as to be enticing! He smiled. She was delightful and full of surprises.

He bowed to her, placing an imaginary hat over his heart. "I accept with the greatest pleasure, my dear Miss Harrison."

"I—I—I don't know what possessed me. You don't have to accept—"

"Of course I do. I've never been to the parade and now I look forward to seeing it with you."

Alexander watched with pleasure the delicate pink that was dyeing Brenda's cheeks. She was flustered and didn't want to look at him. He was glad she had been impulsive and asked him. For the first time in many months, he felt carefree and young.

"Tell me about our outing." He made himself comfortable in her armchair.

Brenda was relieved he was taking this seriously instead of laughing at her. She tried to ignore the wild joy surging through her. She was being ridiculous and foolish. This date was a novelty to him and, therefore, appealing. It didn't mean he wanted to be with her, per se. But they could have a good time together; not be alone for the holiday.

"The parade starts at one o'clock. We'll go earlier because it'll be hard to find a parking space. There'll be bands and floats and fire engines." Thinking of it, Brenda's eyes sparkled. "After the parade, we'll go to the American Legion place to buy food at the booths or play the games of chance. Across the street is a craft fair."

Alexander realized he didn't know much about the city he had been born in and where his family had their business. True, he had spent more time away from Canfield than in it; still, he should show more interest in the city's activities.

The Tycoon and the Schoolteacher   57

"Does this celebration take place every year?"

"Alexander! Where have you been? Didn't you go to school here?"

Memories of the boarding schools and summer camps surfaced.

"No." He didn't want to explain. After them, had come Oxford and his racing career. He'd chased around the world for thrills and excitement, which he didn't miss at all. His restless spirit was finding some peace as he worked with his uncle in the family business. His father had retired two years ago. At last, he felt he was useful.

"Then we have a date?" Alexander wanted confirmation.

"Can't back out of it," Brenda teased. "I'll pick you up at noon on Saturday."

"Not on your life! I'll—"

"No, sir. You're my date and I'll drive you." Brenda explained, "Your car is too conspicuous. Many strangers come into town for this event and I wouldn't want anything to happen to your expensive car."

Alexander was again reminded she thought of the things that might result in a cost. Though he certainly didn't want his car vandalized, he had ample insurance to cover such a situation and another car to take its place. He wasn't going to argue with her on this score. Since she looked so serious and determined, he'd go along with it. But, ride in her car? He shuddered and then saw the humor of the situation. He gave a chuckle.

"It'll be a treat to have a lady chauffeur. I'll be waiting at my front door."

"Wear jeans and a sport shirt. No one dresses up for this."

"Any other commands, General?"

Brenda smiled back at him. "If you obey all my directives, I'll pack us a picnic lunch. I make delicious fried chicken."

"An offer I can't refuse."

Brenda realized she had been giving orders to her boss and he hadn't fired her. On Saturday, she meant for him to have a day he'd never forget. She hoped no one would recognize him. That's why she wanted to pick him up and told him to wear jeans. She'd protect him from becoming a news item on TV. Alexander had been hounded during his racing days. She'd do her best not to draw anyone's attention to him.

Since she had been away for eight years, she also hoped she wouldn't run into many of her high school friends. But she wasn't being realistic on that score. Everyone came to the parade and the celebration. It was a tradition to be followed religiously.

On second thought, it would be nice to have the most gorgeous man in the world as her escort. What a coup it would be for the ugly duckling of her class to have a handsome man on whose arm she would cling.

* * *

The Tycoon and the Schoolteacher 59

On the fourth, the sun shone brightly and the temperature was a comfortable seventy-five degrees.

Brenda wore a pair of red shorts, a sleeveless white blouse, and white sandals. Her legs had tanned nicely during her weekends of sun bathing. A red ribbon secured her pony tail.

She remembered to put sunscreen on her nose to prevent a burn. She thought of Alexander's deep tan. And wondered where he had acquired it.

It was easy to picture him on a sunny beach or on a sail boat—or would it be a yacht? Hardly alone, though. She didn't want to think he'd have someone special with him.

When Brenda got out of the car and came around to open the passenger door for him, Alexander gave a low whistle. "Very, very nice. I think I'll hire you to be my permanent chauffeur."

Brenda blushed and smiled. She was going to surrender to all her fantasies about being Cinderella and seeing her prince. There wasn't going to be a 12:00 limit to the day's festivities.

"Are you going to demand to drive?" Brenda asked. She shrugged her shoulders and started to get into the passenger seat.

Alexander stopped her.

"You're my chauffeur for today. My nerves will handle the experience." A big grin lit up his face.

Brenda gave an "Umph" and got behind the wheel. Although Alexander looked as though he applied the imaginary brakes several times, he made no critical

60 *Ludima Gus Burton*

remarks. Nor did he make a crack about riding in her old car. When she pulled into town, she ignored his loud sigh of relief.

After going up and down several streets, Brenda found a parking space. They walked from it to Main Street. She spoke to a number of people who expressed their pleasure of seeing her again after all these years. Alexander noted the looks of curiosity thrown his way. Brenda didn't introduce him; she kept them moving.

He asked quietly, "Are you ashamed to be with me?"

"Heavens, no! I'm protecting your identity so you aren't bothered by the news media. See that reporter and camera over there? If I don't give your name, they can only speculate. Don't you agree?"

"Thank you. It's perfect with me. If you do have to introduce me, just call me Alex Gregory—my middle name—and leave off the Stone."

"Ah, so for today, I have the honor?"

Alexander looked discomforted, but nodded his head.

"Okay, Alex. This is a good spot to watch the parade." Brenda put her arm through his and pulled him close to her side. His gaze made her feel warm all over. This was truly going to be a day as far removed from the Stone Estate as Cinderella could make it.

"Oh, oh, listen. I hear the school band!" Brenda poked her head out to look down the street. "Here they come. Oh, how I love a parade!"

The Tycoon and the Schoolteacher   61

Down the street came the parade. The American Legion members proudly carried the flags. Everyone placed his hand over his heart in respect for the flag of the country. A lump formed in Alexander's throat at the show of patriotism. Then the bands from many groups, the Boy and Girl Scouts, the proud little Brownies, the baton twirlers, and the clowns marched enthusiastically. What they lacked in talent and finesse, they made up for in joy and spirit. The decorations on the floats were amateurish and simple, but their occupants swelled with pride. The horns and sirens of the many fire engines filled the air. Each unit was heartily cheered and everyone's hands tingled and turned red from the clapping. Candy was thrown all along the way.

"Hurry, Alex, get some candy. You can give it to this little boy who isn't fast enough to get it."

Alexander dove for the candy and came back with a handful. The little boy's smile shone from ear to ear and he shouted with glee to have it.

The horse riders, with their silver-trimmed saddles shining in the sun and the horses prancing with spirit, brought up the rear.

Regrettably, in no time, the parade was over for this year.

The spectators wended their way up the street to where the kiddie amusement park rides, games of chance, and food booths were ready to receive the happy throng.

"Wasn't it wonderful, Alex? I think it was one of the best I've seen. What did you like best?"

Alexander looked down at Brenda's animated, upturned face. He leaned down and lightly kissed her cheek.

"Watching you."

His kiss and compliment took Brenda's breath away. This was truly the stuff of fairy tales. She had to remember, however, that it was only for today. Though her fairy godmother hadn't given her a midnight deadline, she'd give it to herself.

Alexander took her hand and said, "Lead on, Macduff. We have many unknown worlds for me to conquer and experience."

They played some of the so-called games of skill in which Alexander, after a large outlay of money, finally won a tiny teddy bear for Brenda. He hooked a ring over one of the milk bottles for it. They visited the craft show. There, too, he insisted on buying her an Indian necklace of turquoise. Since he said he never owned one, she bought him a red bandanna scarf and tied it around his neck.

"There. You look like a cowboy."

He had taken it in stride.

Her picnic lunch was eaten at one of the tables set out in the city park.

"You're right. Best fried chicken I've ever eaten." He patted his stomach. "Of course, it helps to be as hungry as I am."

The Tycoon and the Schoolteacher   63

Brenda threw a marshmallow at him and scored a direct hit on his forehead.

In the early evening they sat on the grass and enjoyed the patriotic concert given in the small bandstand. With everyone, they oh'd and ah'd at the fireworks which brought the festivities to a close.

At midnight, Cinderella drove her prince home.

Although she asked him to drive, he refused.

"You did okay this morning. My nerves will survive a ride at night."

Brenda had the feeling Alexander's nerves were being frazzled, but he wasn't going to show it to her. She stopped before the front door of the mansion, her car making itself heard and shattering the quiet of the countryside.

"Good night, Alexander—"

"Hey, I thought I was Alex." He made no move to leave the car.

She didn't know what to do next.

Seeing Brenda getting flustered, Alexander reached over and pulled her into his arms. His head descended and his warm lips met hers. His kiss was firm and lasted until she was out of breath. With her shuddering intake of breath, Alexander laughed and let her go.

"I always kiss good night," he said. "Call me when you get home so I'll know you arrived safely."

Cinderella returned to her hearth, bemused and floating on air.

Chapter Seven

After he received the phone call from Brenda saying she had reached her apartment safely, Alexander found it difficult to fall asleep. It had gone against his upbringing to let her drive home alone. It was his responsibility to take care of her and make sure of her safety. Since he was her date, she had been determined to do everything. What a novel experience for him—a woman escorting him. His Brenda was full of surprises.

His Brenda? Whoa, nix on that thought right now. Not for him, and not for her, either. But she had given him one of the happiest days of his life. Every minute was filled with activities he had never participated in before.

How would she act on Monday? It didn't seem pos-

The Tycoon and the Schoolteacher   65

sible that they would still be as relaxed with each
other. Back they would go to their respective stations
in life. Yet the differences seemed to have leveled out
somewhat because of their day together. It made him
feel good about it.

The next day, Brenda recalled every enjoyable
event. She thought Alexander had enjoyed himself. He
was so easy to be with, she forgot most of the time
that he was her wealthy boss and world playboy. She
had introduced him to her friends who acted surprised
to see their former classmate with a hunk.

Definitely, Alexander, her Alex for the day, had
been all she dreamed of.

She wouldn't see him until Monday. By then, he
would be Alexander Stone. She doubted she would
ever have another day in which to call him Alex and
bask in his warm friendship.

Her Aunt Margaret had taught her well to face facts
and not be led astray by daydreams. Dreaming was
fine as long as she understood it was only a dream.
The danger came if she lost sight of reality and let
herself drift rudderless on the sea of make-believe.

Brenda didn't see Alexander on Monday. A business trip to San Francisco kept him away for a week.
She tried to ignore her disappointment and worked on
the book.

The pièce de résistance of the collection, in Building
One, was the UNI Taxi, 1908, designed to meet Lon-

don's strict police specifications. With very little alteration, the car remained in production for twenty years. Brenda thought that many modern cars were fortunate to see a ten-year life span.

It was easy to learn that speed, from the beginning, was an obsession of car manufacturers. Merciful heavens, one hundred miles an hour was officially broken as early as July, 1904!

So, she mused, when Philip put his foot to the accelerator and Alexander flew around the race track, they were doing "what-came-naturally!" No wonder Philip had laughed at her attempts to slow him down. The desire to speed, to have the wind tear through his longish hair, to thumb his nose at danger, was in his DNA! Speed—the faster, the better.

Alexander was no different. He showed no signs of slowing down, albeit on his private track instead of the international circuit. And why should he slow down at her request? She hadn't any influence in his life. The only males she had any influence over were those who were in her classes—and under eighteen.

On Friday, Brenda walked down the line of cars. Stuck in the corner was a car she hadn't noticed before. She pushed aside the branches of the plant. She gasped, all air leaving her lungs.

There, in all of its restored glory, was Gramps's roadster!

No, not Gramps's, but one just like it.

She recalled her grandfather taking her hand and

The Tycoon and the Schoolteacher   67

leading her to the old barn which pitched to one side, waiting for gravity to pull it down in a heap.

Gramps pushed aside the protesting door and showed her the car.

"This, Little Missy, was the first car I bought in 1926. It's a Chandler roadster. The company doesn't exist anymore. Oh," he gave a sigh and his faded blue eyes misted, "I was a king when I drove this car. It cost five times more than the other cars of that day."

"Oh, Gramps, take me for a ride!"

Her grandfather gave a hearty laugh and entered into her make-believe world.

"Here, I want you to ride in the rumble seat."

He pulled up the top of the trunk and there, inside, was a bench seat with a padded back. He quickly dusted away some of the cobwebs. Her grandfather showed her how to use the step on the fender to climb in.

He got behind the wheel and the motor roared into their world of imagination, the wind blowing in her face and whipping her long black hair in a stream behind her . . .

Brenda sank into a heap in front of the restored car and covered her face with her hands. The tears seeped between her fingers and sobs shook her shoulders. Oh, Gramps, I miss you so much.

When another picture crept into her mind, her tears slowly stopped. Her eyes saw Alexander and herself singing joyously as the Chandler roadster roared down the road, her bridal veil and long hair streaming over the open rumble seat with its JUST MARRIED sign. Behind the car, the string of old shoes and tin cans bounced merrily over the rough pavement . . .

Brenda swiped the last of the tears from her cheeks with the back of her trembling hand. She gave a rueful laugh.

Brenda, Brenda, you are a sentimental fool. Wake up—again—to the reality of your life.

Alexander was never going to marry her and that beautiful Chandler car was never going to leave its exalted place in the showroom to drive along a modern highway. This car, and all the others, were on their hallowed carpets for the rest of their days.

On sudden impulse, she pulled on the handle of the rumble seat. With her heart pounding, she climbed in. Closing her eyes, it was easy to imagine a real ride in it. To dream of cuddling with Alexander in the chilly air . . .

With a sigh, she got out. Perhaps she could somehow incorporate her experience about riding in the rumble seat in the book. She wouldn't name herself, of course. She felt just like the movie producer, Alfred Hitchcock, who had to be in every one of his movies. Then, this would be her book as well as one for Alexander's parents.

She was happy the Chandler was in the Stone Collection. It was as though there was a connection between her past and Alexander's present. Dared she believe fate had brought her here to write the book?

Tired of writing about the vintage cars, Brenda de-

The Tycoon and the Schoolteacher   69

cided to work in Showroom Two where the classic cars were housed.

She already planned to divide the book into two parts: Vintage cars, 1886 to 1954 and Classic cars, 1954 to 1978. The vintage part had twenty cars.

She shuffled through the photographs of the remaining thirty in the Classic period and stuffed them into a folder. She grabbed her clipboard. Walking out of her office, she ran full-tilt into Alexander's hard chest as he stood in the doorway.

"Whoa, what's the hurry?" he asked. He set her away from him.

"You're back! I'm glad." A radiant smile curved Brenda's lips. "Did you have a good trip?"

Her warm welcome filled him with pleasure.

"Very, but it's good to be home again." He wanted to add, to be seeing you.

"I'm off to the other building," Brenda explained. "I'm tired of looking at the vintage cars and need to get inspired with the other cars."

"I personally like the classic cars. Must be because they're more stylish. I like the new ideas of the manufacturers." He said with a grin, "I'll bet you don't know that, although the British were first with the sports car and the coupe, it was we Americans who came up with the machines that were literally all things to all men. They went from chrome and tail fins to bucket seats, center consoles, and floor-shifters."

"A succinct history of the American market in one sentence! You should be writing this book."

"No! That's your job and I'll leave you to it." He turned and left her.

His abrupt departure caught Brenda by surprise. For some reason, any writing suggestion on her part elicited such a response. What unhappy incident in his schooling had the power to affect a highly successful tycoon so many years later? Should she stop reminding him to write his dedication? On this point, she was standing firm. He had to write it himself.

Brenda entered Showroom Two.

The impressive collection had its impact on her. If only she could make the cars come alive. She had to leave out the technical stuff about engines and put in the facts that were interesting from a woman's point of view, like the color of the seats, or that the early cars had no roofs, and all the clothes and veils a woman had to wear. For some reason, she felt it was especially important to Alexander's happiness to have his mother cherish his gift. She figured his father already knew the dull engineering facts about the insides of a car engine.

The housekeeper sent down her lunch each day. Sometimes Alexander joined her. He wasn't around every day as he had been in the beginning. He went into the office to work on the fall promotion of the new cars to be sold in the company's showrooms. He was also busy with the car he wanted to enter in the April International Car Show.

April.

The Tycoon and the Schoolteacher   71

She would be long gone out of his life. She'd learn the results from the news media. She hated to think of never seeing him again.

She hid from him her interest. Interest was a good word to cover up the strong feelings she didn't want to acknowledge even to herself. Not saying the word love aloud prevented it from floating out into the universe to finally invade Alexander's consciousness.

Alexander slid out on a dolly from under his red sports car. Grease streaked his blond hair and forehead. He was muttering under his breath. Brenda suspected that he was swearing.

"What's wrong?" she asked.

"Would you understand my explanation if I told you?"

"Probably not. But I can give you my sympathy."

"That's not enough. Suffice it to say, I'm having trouble with that 'slight adjustment' you once told me I could do so easily."

"You're actually making your car woman-attractive? I can't believe it."

"Trying, is the operative word. It would have been easier if such a consideration was part of the original blueprints." He smiled ruefully.

"Is this the car you're entering in the competition? I'm sure you'll win because it will be so unusual."

Alexander gave a hoot of laughter. "I only wish you were one of the judges."

There was no scorn in his gaze, only warm gaiety.

72   *Ludima Gus Burton*

Brenda felt her heart fill with an unreasonable happiness. So she was making a difference. She was helping Alexander expand his vision.

Alexander picked up the special pliers he needed and sunk back on the dolly.

"Back to work," he said and disappeared under the car.

"Bye, I'll see you again," Brenda said above the noise that now issued from under the car. She left the garage with a light step.

The unnecessary hammering which Alexander had made had nothing to do with his adjustment to the car. Frustration struck the blows. He should never have listened to Brenda's suggestion. She knew little about cars and shouldn't be telling him what to do. Why had he decided, against all his engineering instincts, to consider such a drastic overhaul of his basic design? It was more than a seat adjustment. That was the rather easy one. Would he be able to make his man's sports car a woman's car as well, and still not be laughed out of the show? More and more, he doubted it.

Brenda was making him change and he didn't like it. If only she wouldn't look at him with her big eyes full of helpful intentions. He found himself wanting to be near her, to see her every day, to have her smile at him. Even now he wanted to chase after her and use the excuse that he wanted to see what more she had written on the book.

The book.

Had the gods-that-be planted the idea in his head so

The Tycoon and the Schoolteacher   73

Brenda would enter his life? Had they arranged for Uncle Charles to accidently meet her at the Library Fund Raiser? He had never believed in fate, but it could be a possible force working in his life this summer. His summer that had been turned upside down by a schoolteacher who made him feel as emotional as a high-school student.

Before Brenda entered his life, he had had his summer and fall planned and organized. He would spend days in the office making sure the company's promotions would be financially successful.

His competition sports car was off the assembly line on time for him to spend the months needed to perfect it. He wanted to enter the field of sports car design as a viable contender on his own merits—not on his past reputation as a race car driver. His success had been due largely to the personal adjustments he had made to his cars—cars made by others.

This entry car was his alone, from the blueprint design to the actual model. His alone—until he let Brenda become a co-designer! What had he been thinking? And now he was at the point of no return. He had to go forward and make the necessary changes. And, by god, the color would remain red and not pink!

He had to admit, grudgingly, that his car would be a new concept at the car show. He was going to be branded a traitor to his hard-core compatriots. Already, he could hear the roar of their disapproval. Hopefully, the public would applaud.

*   *   *

The beautiful, lazy days of summer were flying by. Brenda found it hard to write all the pages which she scheduled in the morning. Now she could understand how difficult it had been for her students to write their assignments.

The outline to the book had been the easiest part. Deciding what cars to write about and how much research to include had been harder than she had anticipated. What if she couldn't do it? And having Alexander demanding to see her progress each week had been nerve wracking.

"Don't breathe down my neck," she exclaimed one Friday afternoon in early August. His spicy aftershave was tantalizing her and she could feel the warmth of his body. "I'm going as fast as I can. I don't work in a chronological order. I do bits and pieces of pages as they come to me. Later, I'll pull it all together."

"Not very logical to me," he criticized.

"I just typed twenty-five pages which I'll print out to show you."

Brenda swung back to her keyboard, irritated and tired. Tears of frustration blurred her vision. Her elbow hit the power key and wiped out her typed pages.

Chapter Eight

"Oh, no! I've wiped out today's work!"

"Brenda, I'm sorry—"

"It's not your fault, but—go back to your little cars and leave me to retype the pages."

She turned her back to him and her fingers flew on the keyboard.

Though he would rather put his arms around her and console her, Alexander made a strategic retreat. He remembered Brenda didn't need his constant prodding. He was pleased with her progress on the book. She'd easily overcome this little set-back.

After Alexander left, Brenda laid her head down on the edge of the keyboard. What a stupid thing to do. She had thought she had been saving the pages all along, but her thoughts were too often on Alexander and not on the mundane job of word processing. All those precious pages. She'd never be able to recall the exact words and sentences.

She raised her head, reached for her research notebook, and went to page one of the lost section. She'd work all afternoon and into the night to do them over while the material was still fresh in her mind. A full weekend away from the material would kill her.

At 6:00, she became conscious that it was very quiet on the compound. She got up and stretched. It felt good to stand up. She went to the door. The garage doors were closed. Only her car was in the parking area. Alexander had left, too.

Good. She was alone and able to work as long as she wanted. She had ten more pages and she wasn't going to stop until she did them, no matter how late it got to be.

The utter quiet was eerie. Though scoffing at her fears, Brenda locked the office door. With her back to it, she felt better about not being surprised by an unwanted intruder. She rubbed her eyes and went back to her manuscript.

At sundown Alexander parked his car before the front door of his house. He'd take a quick shower, change, and still have time to meet his Uncle Charles for a late dinner at the club. This Friday meeting with his uncle was one he always looked forward to.

Force of habit had him looking out of the upstairs hall window down to the buildings of the compound.

The Tycoon and the Schoolteacher 77

He turned away and did a double take. Brenda's car was still there. He could also see the light streaming out into the dusk from her office window.

Still working? Then he remembered the lost pages. He'd better check on her. Of course, the entrance gates were locked after 6:00 and no intruder could get in. Still . . .

Alexander hurried out of the house and walked down the hill. She should have left at her usual hour. Just like a woman to be foolish with her physical welfare.

He looked through the door window into the office.

Brenda, seated with her back to the door, was looking at the screen. Her elbow was next to the keyboard while her hand massaged her forehead, unaware of his presence. Her shoulders drooped forward, showing how tired she was.

Furious, Alexander grasped the door knob, ready to burst in and bawl her out. The door didn't open.

At the noise, Brenda turned around, her eyes wide with fright. Her hand went to her mouth and she smothered a scream.

It was only Alexander at the door.

Oh, dear, he looks furious. Well, it is late and getting dark . . .

She unlocked the door.

"Hello," she said and looked at her watch. "Goodness, I had no idea it was so late." She walked back to her computer and carefully hit the save key. "I'll be ready to leave in a minute."

Alexander wasn't mollified at her attempt at lightness. He scowled at her. "At least you had the sense to lock the door. But don't do this again. If you feel you have to work late, I want to be notified. Do you hear me?"

"Yes, sir," Brenda answered, lowering her eyelids and dipping her head meekly, suddenly feeling mischievous.

Alexander was surprised she didn't make a deep curtsy to him. A smile nudged at the corners of his mouth at the thought. When she looked up at him through her long lashes, he thought she was trying to tease him.

He gazed into her beautiful eyes; he stopped breathing.

She gazed up at him; her breath caught in her throat.

He wanted desperately to pull her into his arms and kiss her as he had been longing to do since the first time he saw her.

She wished she had the courage to pull his face down to hers, to place her lips on his.

He did nothing.

She lost her courage.

And the moment for action was lost.

Brenda sighed and turned to cover her computer.

"Please don't do this again," he repeated his order.

"No, sir, never again," she promised as her heart continued to skip a beat at the concern in his voice.

The Tycoon and the Schoolteacher   79

"If you give me a lift to the house, I'll follow you home."

"You don't have to—"

"I'll feel better if I see you home safely." He folded his long frame into the passenger seat.

"I can take care of myself," Brenda protested. "It isn't late—"

"Don't argue with me, Brenda."

Irritated with him, she stepped hard on her brakes when she came before the front door of the house. The unexpected move sent Alexander against the dashboard. He rubbed his knee and muttered under his breath.

"You should have put on your seat belt," Brenda said innocently. "Did you hurt your knee, Alex?"

"Alexander."

"Yes, sir, Alexander, sir."

Alexander pursed his lips and didn't answer her. He got into his car, made a great show of putting on his seat belt and motioned her to drive ahead of him.

Brenda snickered. She found his actions endearing. It felt good to be looked after. She drove her car into town and into her assigned space.

Alexander parked behind her. This was the first time he had come to her apartment. He found the surroundings dreary and littered with refuse. The apartment building, however, had had a new coat of paint and looked clean and respectable.

"Is it always this dark?"

"No. The pole light has burned out. I'll report it to the super."

At the front door of the apartment building, Brenda turned to Alexander. "Thank you."

"Your key," he demanded.

Brenda knew better than to protest. For some reason, Alexander had made up his mind to see her enter her apartment.

She shouldn't put much store into his actions. There was no possibility Alexander had any personal feelings for her. It was just his overwhelming sense of responsibility which made him protective of all his employees. They had told her of his interest in their personal family problems, the payment of medical bills, and extra bonuses.

"I live on the third floor. There is no elevator," Brenda explained. Her gaze went to the stairs and she was thankful they were clean.

Although Alexander's eyebrows went up, he didn't make a comment. He motioned for her to proceed up the stairs. He admired her long legs without guilt.

"Not much light," he criticized.

"I'm used to it. It really is a safe building," she defended. It was one reason she was willing to pay the higher rent for the small studio apartment.

After he unlocked the door and threw it open, Brenda asked, "Will you come in? I can make you a cup of coffee."

Much as Alexander wanted to accept, he refused.

The Tycoon and the Schoolteacher   81

"I'm having dinner with Uncle Charles. Another time. Good night."

He started to walk away. Over his shoulder he ordered, "Go inside, Brenda, and lock the door."

Brenda shut the door and shot the bolt. Only then did she hear Alexander's footsteps fade away on the stairs.

She slumped against the door, trying to understand her mixed feelings. Annoyed at Alexander for all his orders; yet longing to have him show personal interest in her. She was exhausted, but glad to be home safe and sound, thanks to the efforts of her employer. That was the operative word—her employer—and not her Prince Charming.

It was a good thing he hadn't come inside. He would have seen the great difference between their living arrangements.

A compact kitchen gave her just enough room to reach the refrigerator, stove and sink by merely turning around in one spot. The door to the right led to her equally small bathroom. A counter separated the kitchen from the rest of the apartment. Two high stools were in front of it.

A sofa bed, an easy chair with a big square footstool, a long coffee table, and two end tables with pink shades on the lamps took up three-quarters of the room. A long table against the inner wall was her desk. Beneath it were bookshelves crowded with stacks of books.

82   *Ludima Gus Burton*

Alexander would feel squashed in this apartment. She was glad he hadn't accepted her offer to come in.

She was tempted to break her promise not to work late as the deadline came closer and closer.

On the first of August, she advertised for a second-hand computer that would be compatible with the one in the office. When she was able to buy one, she was able to work at home and conceal from Alexander the actual hours she was working. She had almost bitten off more than she could chew. Almost, but not quite. She was doing it, even though she had to write as many hours at home as she did in the Estate office.

Her biggest difficulty was deciding what cars she would showcase. Most of these were found in Buildings Two and Three, those called the Classic cars.

The 1954 Chevrolet Corvette was America's first sports car, a dream car with a fiber-glass body. She had to write about it for Alexander's sake!

The one that fascinated Brenda was the 1959 Ford Fairlane Skyliner because it was the wackiest car to come out of Detroit. After she saw it, Brenda ran to get Alexander. She dragged him to the car.

"Alexander, please, show me how this roof top retracts. I'm afraid to do it."

"I don't blame you. I'll show you."

"Wow!" she said after he demonstrated. "To think you have this car in your collection. Your father will want to be reminded of it!" She grabbed Alexander's arm and squeezed it. "Oh, Alexander, you had the best

The Tycoon and the Schoolteacher   83

idea for a gift when you decided to have this book written."

Alexander looked into Brenda's enraptured, happy face. He wanted to keep the joy always shining in her, to make her as excited about everything he did.

Brenda was already leading him to another one of her favorites. Today she had the need to have him with her, not have him read about it later.

Because of his racing history, she wanted him to see it through her eyes. A 1966 Chevrolet Corvette Sting Ray, the most collectable of them all.

"I tried to get my grandfather to let me drive this car, but he said, absolutely no!"

Brenda sighed as she looked down the line of re-maining cars. "I wish I lived when these cars were actually being driven on our roads. What a thrill even you would have. Cars today are so boring."

"Hey, you mean mine are boring?"

Brenda was immediately contrite. "No, no. You're the exception. I'm sure, years from now, yours will be collectables, because they are unique."

"Please!" Alexander threw up his hands in mock horror. "Don't make me a great-grandfather before my time. I'll be happy to sell my cars today so people can enjoy them." He gestured to the cars in the showroom. "These are never going to be ridden again and it's sad in a way."

Brenda thought of the Chandler roadster and her dream of riding in it. He was right, of course. The collection was for people to look at and admire and that was all.

"Thanks for showing me how that roof retracted and for letting me rave on and on," Brenda said. "I won't keep you any longer from your work."

"My pleasure," Alexander said, and he smiled down at Brenda. He didn't want to leave her. Every day he found it harder to stay away. He had to keep remembering why she was here—the book.

"How's the photographer doing? Will he have the pictures done when you want them?"

"He's wonderful. We're grouping some of the cars, the ones that are colorful but have only interesting mechanical facts about them. I want the book to be interesting to your mother and not just to your father."

"Right. I trust you to make the decisions."

"Don't forget you have to do your dedication."

Alexander seemed to freeze. The happy animation in his face disappeared. "I'll get it to you soon," he said, and promptly left her alone.

Remorse gripped Brenda. Alexander didn't want to write the dedication.

Then it hit her.

She was an English teacher and he expected her to correct his effort, to tear it apart and tell him to do it over and over again.

Two days later, Alexander came to the office. Brenda wasn't there and he felt the disappointment as

The Tycoon and the Schoolteacher   85

a real pain. He glanced into the showroom and saw a spot of red in the far corner. He hurried toward it.

Brenda had her hand on the hood of a blue Chandler. The wistfulness and longing in her gaze twisted Alexander's heart. He wondered what she was thinking.

She turned to Alexander, not surprised to see him. There had been other times when he had materialized because of her thoughts of him.

"I love this car," she said, her hand lovingly stroking it. "What a thrill it must have been to ride in it. A woman would feel like a queen—with her king beside her, of course."

With a start, Brenda realized she had spoken her thoughts aloud. How silly it must sound to Alexander. She could feel the heat of a violent blush sweeping over her neck and face. She put her hands on her cheeks and refused to look at Alexander.

He gently pulled her hands down and held them.

"Don't ever be embarrassed to voice a beautiful sentiment," he said. "Why is this car special to you?"

"The first car my grandfather bought was a Chandler like this one. He could never make himself get rid of it. He had it stored in a barn on his farm. When I came here and saw yours, all the memories came flooding back."

"Anytime you want to see it, you can come back," Alexander teased. "We'll never get rid of it and we'll keep it especially for you."

86   *Ludima Gus Burton*

"Thank you, kind sir." Brenda dropped him a curtsy. "Were you looking for me?"

"I heard from the printer. He's ready whenever you are."

"Your dedication—"

"Right here." Alexander gave the handwritten sheet to her. Brenda read it slowly and carefully.

This book is dedicated to my loving and loved parents. You have been there for me through all my years. You will always live deep in my grateful heart.

"Is it acceptable?" he asked.

Brenda's eyes were moist with unshed tears. She shook her head. "Alexander, it's beautiful—just right. It needs no improvement—and I speak as an English teacher!"

The smile which lit up Alexander's face almost blinded Brenda. She was so happy for him. This book was truly going to be a memorable gift in every way. She only wished she could be there when he gave it to his mother and father. She wanted to see their reaction and their expression of love.

"I'll contact the printer." Brenda said, "As they say, 'all systems are go.' "

Bound in rich mahogany-colored leather, the large book, ten inches by eight inches, had one hundred and fifty pages, tipped with gold leaf. The title, *The Stone*

The Tycoon and the Schoolteacher 87

Collection of Vintage and Classic Cars, was in gold. The colored photographs were works of art. Brenda didn't attempt to guess at the cost of its limited edition of only fifty copies.

When Alexander presented her with her copy, Brenda's eyes widened in surprise. Her name, as author, was below the title. Alexander must have ordered the printer to do this without her knowledge.

Her first published book! Tears filled her eyes.

"I didn't expect you to put my name on the cover."

"Of course your name had to be on it." He went on, "I can't find the words to express my appreciation for making this book exactly what I hoped for."

To further her emotional agitation, Alexander said, "Please autograph my copy."

"I'll be happy to."

Silence fell between them. Brenda suddenly realized her job was finished. No longer would she be coming to the Estate office which felt like it belonged to her. No longer would she see the beautiful gardens and hear the birds singing their joyous songs. No longer would she see Alexander almost every day. All she would have would be her memories.

Brenda broke the silence. "Since the book is finished, my work here is done. I'm even two weeks early. I'll have a vacation before my teaching job starts September first."

"Do you want to go back to teaching?" Alexander asked. "Wouldn't you rather write, pick your own hours—"

"Oh, Alexander, you don't get it! I don't have a trust fund to pay the rent and buy my food while I sit at a computer waiting for words to come to me. I have to work and earn money."

"Right. Sorry." Alexander flushed with embarrassment. "It's going to be strange to have you gone. I've—we've—gotten used to having you in and out of the buildings." He went on, "May I take you out to dinner on Friday night at the Castlerock Restaurant? We'll celebrate the book."

"I'd like that," Brenda accepted after a moment of hesitation. The invitation had taken her by surprise.

"I'll pick you up at seven."

Chapter Nine

The table was in one of the alcoves. The circular window overlooked a formal garden with a full moon casting its silvery magic. Soft music played in the background, old romantic tunes which Brenda remembered were her aunt's favorites.

She wore a dark red silk sheath. Her grandmother's black lace shawl, embroidered with red roses and bordered with a heavy fringe, was tossed over her bare shoulders. Some of her hair had been piled high and was secured with two Spanish combs; the rest hung down her back. Large gold hoops replaced her gold studs.

She was pleased with the Spanish look. It made her look different from the golden blond beauties Alexander usually dated.

Alexander was entranced.

"You're lovely tonight," he told her, and his fascination with her transformation shone in his eyes.

They talked and laughed, finding many common interests. Alexander toasted Brenda for her excellent book.

"That first day I didn't think you could write this book. You proved me very wrong."

Brenda glowed with his praise. This was a night to remember in the coming months.

He went on, "I still think you should consider writing as a full-time profession. Besides, Hilliard High School is no place for you."

"Alexander, listen to me. I'm a teacher and I love it. I don't want to do anything else full time. I've worked all my life to become a teacher and I'm happy with my choice."

"That may be, but—"

"Please, let's not talk about it anymore. It's getting late. Perhaps we should leave."

For her the evening was spoiled. Alexander didn't understand her at all. She had been fooling herself all summer.

"I'm sorry," Alexander apologized, "I didn't mean to upset you—"

"It's all right. I've had a lovely evening but I'd like to go home now."

Alexander was perplexed. What had he done? Would he ever understand her?

Brenda flung her shawl about her shoulders and

The Tycoon and the Schoolteacher   91

wended her way between the tables to the exit. She waited for Alexander to settle the bill.

He took her by the elbow and escorted her out. She didn't break the silence between them as they waited for his car to be brought to the steps.

Her thoughts tumbled over and over. How could she have been so wrong? Easy. She had had stardust in her eyes and fancies in her brain and hadn't faced the reality in her life.

A man like Alexander would never be able to understand being without great wealth. He'd always been able to do whatever he wanted because he had the money. Even today, he could indulge himself with his sports cars. If they weren't successful, he would go on to something else and not have to worry about paying the rent or having medical insurance or buying food.

Look at the expensive gift he was giving his parents—she shuddered to think of the cost—on the best paper, having colored illustrations and leather binding. Her salary during the summer must have been a small item in the cost.

But greater than the differences in their economic stations was the gulf between them in career aspirations. She had had to fight every step of the way to become a certified teacher. He had waltzed into his family's business and been given a CEO position. Sure, she acknowledged, begrudgingly, he was working night and day to win a place in the world for his car designs. So they did share a like passion for something . . .

Still, it was a good thing the book was finished, and so was her professional relationship with him.

Brenda looked at Alexander and saw a puzzled frown on his face. He looked upset. She was sorry she had spoiled the evening he had planned for her. She had to make him feel happier.

"When will you give the book to your parents?"

Alexander was happy to be talking again. "I'll be leaving on Wednesday. The anniversary is September tenth. I'll stay two weeks with them."

"Ah, you'll be there during my vacation. We'll both be starting back to work at the same time."

"Yes."

Brenda wondered what else he would have said if they hadn't reached her apartment. They sat, not saying anything, and staring straight ahead.

This was good-bye and Brenda felt frozen in her seat. How was she going to say the difficult words—without crying?

Alexander's hand went to his breast pocket and he started to pull out a long slender box. He had bought a diamond bracelet which he wanted to give to Brenda as a farewell gift. At the dinner he realized that it would have been his biggest mistake. Brenda wasn't like the women in his past. She'd have been insulted by such a gift. He was glad he realized in time. He was in enough hot water as it was. He still felt he was right about her writing and about Hilliard High School. The reports about the school were bad and he was worried about her safety. But Brenda didn't see

The Tycoon and the Schoolteacher   93

his point and made no bones about telling him to mind his own business.

Brenda released her seat belt. Alexander quickly got out and came around to her door. They walked up the stairs to her apartment.

"I wish you a good trip, Alexander." Brenda hunted for the right words. "I've loved writing the book and I had a wonderful summer. Thank you so much."

A wry smile was Alexander's answer. "Good-bye, Brenda. When I get back, I'll call you."

He took the key from her hand and opened the door. "Get inside," he ordered.

Brenda gave him one last look and disappeared inside. Alexander shut the door with a snap.

She listened to his footsteps down the stairs. A moment later, she heard the uncharacteristic screech of tires when Alexander accelerated and was gone.

Brenda pulled out the two combs and tossed her head. He was gone, gone out of her life. He would never call her. How cold and distant were their last sentences—as though they were total strangers.

She wondered what had been in the box he had returned to his breast pocket. A farewell gift? If so, why hadn't he given it to her? A bracelet? A diamond bracelet, the usual gift to women he dated? Thank heavens, if that were so, he hadn't insulted her by giving it to her. He had some sense. She had done her job and had been paid handsomely for it. No other payment was necessary. But it would have been nice to receive a little gift to remember him by. For a minute, she thought he was going to kiss her. If only he had.

Looking around her apartment she noted that the only framed picture was one of her Aunt Margaret. She picked it up and ran her hand over her cheek and caressed it. Pictures helped to keep one's memories accurate. All she had now were memories of Alexander and time would distort them. His features would become hazy and fade away entirely.

She should have taken a camera on that long ago Fourth of July outing. She should have taken pictures of a laughing, happy Alex.

But there were pictures of him in magazines.

She found one in an old issue of *People* magazine. There he was, standing beside one of his race cars. He was smiling, his eyes narrowed against the bright sunlight. His hair was being blown by the wind. This was the picture for her. She could dream he was smiling at her . . .

Though feeling very foolish, Brenda cut and fitted the picture into a frame. She put it on the coffee table at the opposite corner from Aunt Margaret. It was easy to imagine that they smiled at each other—and at her.

The room suddenly seemed brighter and less lonely.

Though thoughts of Alexander and her summer kept coming back to her like a song a person can't get out of one's mind, the two weeks sped by. She looked in vain for even a postcard from Alexander. She'd have

The Tycoon and the Schoolteacher 95

sent him one . . . More and more she was sure she'd never hear from him, let alone see him.

As the first day of school grew closer, a growing premonition assailed Brenda that the coming year wasn't going to be pleasant. For one thing, she hadn't asked enough questions or insisted on visiting the school during school hours. Her interview had been on a Saturday morning because she didn't want to take a day off. Very satisfying at that time, but from the reports she had heard and the sights she had seen when she drove by the building, she hadn't known the true state of affairs. If she had, she probably never would have accepted the one-year contract to teach tenth-grade English.

But, did the fates decide she had to come so she would meet Alexander? She had to stop such a ridiculous train of thought. So she had met Alexander. The fates hadn't made him fall in love with her!

Because her old car had to be junked, she took a bus and walked the two blocks to the school. The littered streets were ringed by run-down apartment buildings. Ragged curtains billowed out of open or broken windows. This section of town had gone downhill in the eight years she had been away from Canfield.

On the first day of school, she even wondered if she was witnessing a drug deal only one block away from the high steel-link fence which surrounded the school and playing fields. A shiver shuddered down her spine. She gave a short laugh. It was broad daylight and she would be safe walking.

A new principal, Mr. Haggerty, had been hired to control the unruly students and raise the low scholastic achievement. This was going to be, at the least, an interesting year for her. She needed such a "baptism by fire" if she were to achieve her goal of becoming a principal, a dream she had not forgotten. She had to know what to do in every situation requiring discipline. Hands-on experience was the best teacher.

Brenda walked to the blackboard and wrote her name on top. Mrs. Baird had been popular with her students and she would be a hard act to follow. She looked again at her daily schedule. Five classes in tenth-grade English, two study halls to supervise, and one free period. Mounds of papers to correct.

Why, oh why, had she left Simpson Central School to work in this education sweatshop? One year. If only time would pass as quickly as her months spent on the Stone Estate.

She wondered if Alexander missed her. What a foolish thought. She had written the book he wanted and they would never see each other again. They lived and moved in two different worlds. Already he was enjoying the sunshine and the blue waters of the French Riviera while she occupied a dingy classroom in the old Hilliard building.

Before she drowned in a sea of self-pity and depression, the homeroom bell rang to begin her day and her year. Her spirits rose. She loved teaching and this year would be the challenge she adored. As in Simpson Central School, she vowed to make a difference

The Tycoon and the Schoolteacher   97

in the lives of her young students. She would also be one step closer to her goal, to become a principal before she was thirty—a goal she had never discussed with Alexander.

For the next five school days there had been no time to think about Alexander lolling on the beach in the company of a beautiful woman. On Friday, sitting slumped and exhausted in her bus seat, she tried to put her week behind her. She wanted to escape back to the lazy days of summer. She was paying for the taste of the good life.

The discipline exerted throughout the school by the new principal impressed her. His discipline, but not the man. His eyes were too close together and were dark, bottomless pools. His mouth seldom curved into a smile. His tall, skeleton-thin frame, clothed in a black suit, towered over the students. When his beady gaze was directed at a person, it was enough to intimidate the most foolhardy student. Herself, too!

She had the uneasy feeling that he didn't like her. A silly notion since she had had only five minutes of conversation with him during her lunch hour on the first day. Yet the feeling persisted. Every time she looked up, Mr. Haggerty seemed to be there, observing her. Perhaps he wasn't as impressed with her credentials as the man who hired her. She hoped it was only that. She would prove her worth.

Brenda massaged the back of her neck. Her favorite

class was also her homeroom class. She started and ended the day on a happy note because of them.

She missed Alexander more than she expected. It hurt that she hadn't had a word from him. She thought she had prepared herself for their separation. Not so. Her treacherous heart was at odds with her logical brain.

She recalled their last night. At the beginning, they were in perfect rapport, laughing and talking as though they had been together forever. Then Alexander had spoiled it all—she wouldn't think about it. It was behind her. She had begun a new life, worlds apart from his. Today, the distance was geographical, as well as social.

The Riviera—what a magical place that must be. As soon as she got off the bus in five minutes, she'd be in her small apartment. No sandy beaches and sparkling water for her this weekend. And no Stone Estate or Alexander to go to on Monday either.

At Simpson Central she made it a rule to get all her work done after school, to take no papers home.

Philip had wanted her to himself.

Now, no one waited for her at home and she took papers to correct all the time.

She believed Alexander would be like Philip. He'd demand a woman's full attention and all her time. Unlike Philip, however, he'd have no sympathy for the papers she had to correct. If she hadn't been too busy spinning her daydreams, she would have realized that

The Tycoon and the Schoolteacher   99

he ignored what was important to her. He didn't even see that he might have to change. A woman, today, didn't jump because a man ordered her to.

For two weeks she had been separated from her Prince. A lifetime. Would she always miss him? If only he hadn't suggested she give up her hard-earned career, and understood what drove her. She could then still hope for her happy ending.

His first day back from Europe, Alexander's desk was piled high with back work and his copy of the book written by Brenda. He smiled at it. He would always remember how happy his parents were with his surprise gift.

"Darling, oh, darling, this book is fabulous," his mother cried. "Come, sit between us while we look at every page."

They exclaimed delight and recalled many happy days with his grandfather who had started the collection.

"You'll have to continue the tradition, son," his father said.

Alexander nodded. "Brenda said my cars will be in the collection someday. I told her not to make me a grandfather before my time."

"Brenda?" His mother's eyebrows went up. "Ah, yes, the author of the book. Tell me more about this schoolteacher."

It wasn't until later that Alexander realized he'd given his mother more than facts about Brenda. He remembered the secret smile his mother had shared with his father. Her "We must come home and meet the writer of this wonderful book" took on more significance.

He pushed back the unruly hair from his forehead and shoved aside the business reports. A song from the '40s had been playing on the car radio this morning. Its tune and words came to him in snatches—something about how far he would travel to be where his sweetheart was. Well, for him, not many miles today. He only had to go to Hilliard High School.

Rather than calling Brenda tonight, he was going to her now.

A minute before the bell would ring to end the school day, Brenda heard the squeak of her classroom door opening and the sudden hush in the room. She turned.

"Oh, Miss Harrison," came George's sing-song voice, "here's your boyfriend."

Chapter Ten

Alexander found himself the focus of every eye. The girls giggled and the boys eyed him with interest. Ignoring them, he turned his attention to Brenda.

She didn't look old enough to be a schoolteacher with her braided pony tail, a red blouse tucked into navy blue slacks, and flat pumps.

Brenda felt the slow blush creep over her face at his close perusal. She gazed admiringly at Alexander.

The Mediterranean sun had deepened his tan and bleached his hair. His dark blue business suit emphasized the width of his shoulders and enhanced his air of authority.

Her gaze met his and her welcoming smile matched the one which lit up his face. The classroom with the snickering students fell away. He alone existed in her

102   *Ludima Gus Burton*

universe. She wondered, later, how long she would have made a fool of herself if the bell hadn't rung.

The bell did its work. The students rushed to the door, the girls looked over their shoulders and openly ogled the hunk while the boys admired his wide shoulders.

"Boyfriend." Alexander smiled more broadly. He walked up to her desk.

Brenda's heart beat wildly, but she was able to answer him in a normal voice. "One has to learn to live with adolescent humor. When did you get back? Was the trip all you wanted it to be?"

Alexander wasn't to be turned aside. "Do you have a boyfriend or can I apply for the vacancy?"

"Don't be silly." Brenda tried to hide her breathlessness. She wasn't going to show how much she longed to take his levity seriously.

Alexander's laughter rang out. He persisted. "Answer my question."

"The answer is no—to both parts of your question."

"What a heartless woman you are," Alexander accused. "I've hurried back to see you. I even left my desk piled up with work in order to see you today."

Brenda's gaze was speculative. She couldn't decide how much was truth and how much good-natured banter. Safety lay in believing the latter.

"At least let me take you to Anton's for one of his famous pasta dinners," he requested.

"I'd like that." This was safe ground after the quiv-

The Tycoon and the Schoolteacher   103

ering quicksand. "I'll take these papers home." She shoved the last class's test papers into her briefcase.

Alexander frowned. "Do you always work at home as well as teaching all day? That's not right."

Brenda shook her head. "You haven't a clue about teaching. There's no end to the papers an English teacher has to correct. It can't get done while I'm teaching. So, home it goes." She quickly added, "Don't be sorry for me. I love what I do."

"Leave this job and work for me," he said impulsively. "At least you'll have regular hours and have your evenings free."

"Now you're being silly," Brenda said, stabbed to the core by his offer. He so easily waved aside what was important to her. She hid her disappointment. She wanted to be with Alexander and to enjoy every minute of the evening. They had been apart much too long.

Brenda loved Anton's.

There was no candlelight, no soft music, no privacy. But Brenda felt drawn to Alexander intimately. The barrier of the table between them didn't seem to exist.

They dallied over their cups of coffee and Alexander made no move to leave. Brenda had to say, "Tomorrow is a work day. Better take me home now."

"Always so practical," Alexander teased. "As you command."

After he opened her apartment door and handed her

the key, Brenda thought he would kiss her. He gazed for a long time into her eyes, then stepped away.

"Good night, Brenda."

Entering, she leaned weakly against the closed door and let out the breath she had been holding. She wondered why Alexander had hurried to see her and then he hadn't even tried to kiss her. It didn't make sense.

Alexander paced in front of the fireplace in his living room later that night. He didn't want Brenda to teach in Hilliard High School. He wanted her to be safe from harm. He had never been to a public school. With its peeling walls and unpolished floors, Hilliard dismayed him. Nor had he been in that section of town. The apartment houses with the explicit sex graffiti appalled him. Listless people sat on the stoops while radios and stereos blasted out noise.

Feeling relief, he had driven his car into the protected parking lot reserved for visitors. At least his car wouldn't be vandalized. The principal gave him permission to go to Brenda's room. "The next time, please come after school hours." Alexander took an immediate dislike to the man.

On the way home, he had questioned Brenda about her car.

"It finally chugged its last gasp and I had to junk it."

"How do you get to school? On the school bus?"

"Canfield Bus Company. Teachers can't ride the school bus."

The Tycoon and the Schoolteacher 105

"That's terrible. Let me give you a car."

He hadn't been surprised when she refused the offer.

And the evening had ended on a sour note. He hadn't even kissed her . . .

Two weeks later Brenda's reply to his invitation to dinner was on his answering machine.

"I'm chaperoning the Halloween Dance tonight. Sorry, another time."

With Brenda, it was always "another time." She had more excuses—legitimate ones—than any woman he had ever asked. He couldn't ask her to skip her college classes, could he?

Not tonight.

He would go to her. Besides, she would need a ride home. He shuddered at the thought of her walking through the unsafe streets to her bus stop.

When he parked his Camaro, Alexander groaned. Even within the safety of the school parking lot, he pictured it, on a Halloween night, stripped of its tires, plastered with broken eggs and shaving cream. With a shake of his shoulders, he resigned the car to its fate.

He entered the school and didn't need directions to the gym. The loud and deafening music pierced the gym wall and entered the corridor. He glanced into the darkened gym with its strobe lights. The place was crowded with costumed students.

"Hello, Mr. Stone," sang out a voice at his elbow. A pixie laughed at him. Since she knew his name, she must be in Brenda's homeroom. "Miss Harrison is here, but I won't tell you what she's wearing!" And she was gone into the crowd before he could hold her and get a description from her.

Brenda in costume? In this crowd? But wait, she was a chaperone, so she'd be with the other chaperones. At his school dances at Kinston Military School, the chaperones always stayed together. He looked around. There they were, as far from the loud music as they could get. None of them were in costume. Where was she?

Alexander strode over to the teachers. A Chinese coolie dogged his heels annoyingly. The coolie hung on the fringes of the chaperone phalanx.

"Hello, I'm Alexander Stone. I'm looking for Brenda Harrison. Do you know what she's wearing?"

"Brenda? I didn't know she was here. I haven't seen her. Have you seen her?" The question was thrown to the rest of the group. "Are you sure she's here?"

"One of her students told me she was in costume."

"That accounts for it. One of her classes challenged her to come in costume and that they'd find her in nothing flat."

Greg Martin chuckled. "I don't think they've found her yet. Hope you have better luck."

"I'll wait here and let her find me." Alexander leaned against the wall.

"Excuse me," Alexander apologized when he bumped into the Chinese coolie who was still at his elbow. He shook his head in irritation. Why didn't this

The Tycoon and the Schoolteacher   107

student go back and join the other students in the gym? Probably one of those snoopy students who wanted to listen to the conversation of the chaperones. He turned his back on the student.

The pixie bobbed up in front of him again. "I see you haven't found her," she jeered.

Alexander was too quick for her this time. He grabbed her arm firmly.

"I thought the challenge was that you kids wouldn't find her. You did."

"I'm not in that class, Mr. Stone," the pixie said. "So she's still safe."

"Come on," Alexander coaxed, "tell me what she's wearing."

The pixie was weakening to Alexander's charm. "She's—"

Just then the coolie pushed Alexander forward so that he almost fell against the pixie. He dropped his hold of her. The pixie darted free and was lost in the crowd.

"Damn," he swore under his breath and turned angrily to give the coolie a piece of his mind. The coolie, too, was gone.

Alexander's headache pounded in time with the music. His feet hurt. Why did any sane adult decide to be a teacher? To willingly take a job that required you to endure the torture of chaperoning a school dance seemed crazy to him. What a contrast to his quiet and luxurious office.

*   *   *

108   *Ludima Gus Burton*

The lights came on at twelve o'clock. With Alexander
in their wake, the teachers moved into the gym.

The masks came off.

There was a shout of surprise. The clapping increased as the small coolie was pushed to the front to
win the prize. The pointed hat and mask came off.

Miss Harrison had won the challenge, hands down!

Alexander grinned. He had been fooled. No wonder
the eyes bchind the mask and the black braided pony-
tail had looked familiar. The high heeled shoes and
haughty manner had added inches to her height last
summer. In black flats she only reached his heart.

"We really fooled you, didn't we," crowed the little
pixie. "I'm Annie from her homeroom."

"Yes, you did, but you would have told me if Miss
Harrison hadn't pushed me."

"A miss is as good as a mile," answered Annie.
"You better go up there and claim your girlfriend, Mr.
Stone. Since you're here, my family won't have to
take her home."

All neatly arranged for him, to his great relief.

Alexander went up to Brenda and took her hand.

"Your little friend Annie ordered me to take you
home. What a little tease she is."

Alexander guided her through the crowd. To his
surprise, several of the boys called out, "Good night,
Mr. Stone."

They walked to the door. "Do the boys in your class
remember me from the first time I came to your classroom?"

The Tycoon and the Schoolteacher   109

"Not exactly. After George recognized you, they've been reading up on your racing exploits."

"That's an honor. I thought everyone had forgotten me."

"There was an article and picture of you in this month's *Racing* magazine."

"Do you get that magazine?" Alexander asked. "Hardly your type."

"I get it for the boys. That one, as well as several sport ones. These boys can't afford to get them. The library is limited in their magazine subscriptions."

Alexander was silent. Another reminder of the difference between his wealth and others. Intellectually, he had known this fact, but it was uncomfortable to come face to face with the people affected.

"Is there anything I can do for your class?"

"I'm so glad you asked. I was wondering how to bring up the subject."

For a moment, Alexander experienced disappointment and disillusionment. He was going to be hit for a money contribution.

"The boys want you to come and talk to them," she said. "Please do. It would mean so much to them. They don't get to have a real live celebrity come to the class!"

Alexander felt embarrassed and humble. He was relieved he had been wrong. "Of course, I'll come."

They reached his car. He saw it hadn't suffered any Halloween "fun." He helped Brenda inside. Before she could do it, he fastened her seat belt. When sudden warmth enveloped her at the light touch of his arm across her chest, Brenda stifled her ready protest. Little did he know how much his casual manners and touch affected her.

In the car Alexander asked, "When do you want me to come and what shall I talk about?"

"Your racing days. They're also full of questions about your sports cars. They're taking Auto Mechanics and so their questions will be about that stuff I know nothing about."

Apprehension filled Alexander. "Do you think I can do it? I've never been with teenagers."

"It'll be a piece of cake." Brenda's gaze was full of confidence.

Pleasure warmed Alexander's heart at Brenda's faith in him.

"These are nice kids." She released her seat belt. "I'll call and let you know when. The afternoon will be better, if that's okay with you."

Reaching the door, Brenda turned and asked, "Would you like to come in?"

As before, Alexander refused. "It's late and you must be exhausted. Get to bed as soon as possible."

He bent down and his warm lips brushed her cheek. He was down the stairs before her startled muscles could move.

She touched the spot. Well, it was a kiss—of sorts, to be sure. She'd preferred he did it on her lips.

She wondered whether he had ever before just kissed a woman on the cheek . . .

Not likely.

The Tycoon and the Schoolteacher 111

* * *

Doubt assailed Alexander on the Wednesday he was to go to Brenda's class. What had he gotten himself into? He knew nothing about teenage interests or I.Q.! Would his vocabulary be too difficult, his mechanical information too technical?

Because Brenda didn't talk about difficulties in her teaching, he had thought it was easy. How wrong he was. He had to go through with it. Reluctantly, he put into his briefcase a stack of autographed pictures from his racing days. He hated promoting himself, but he also knew people did want his picture to put in their collections.

Since his sports cars were featured this month in his company's showroom, he slipped these brochures in also. Books on how to design cars and auto mechanics joined the pile. Maybe he wouldn't have to talk much at all; let the boys look at pictures.

Brenda's class of fifteen boys and five girls turned expectant faces to him.

Girls? Five of them. Was this Brenda's way to prove he had to change his ideas? They couldn't know anything about auto mechanics; Brenda didn't. They were there because of his fame and to get an autograph from him. That was okay with him as long as they didn't interfere with his presentation by asking dumb questions.

He was wrong. The girls were as interested and knowledgeable as the boys; in some areas, more so.

They wanted to know about the innovations he made in order to win his races. His present-day sports cars and their mechanics interested them the most. They wanted the nitty-gritty of design and mechanics. Alexander could see some future designers who could one day be his rivals!

The time passed too quickly.

"I'll come back," he promised. Self-consciously, he held up his pictures. "I brought these in case some of you wanted one."

"Yes, I want one," came the request from each one.

Alexander's heart filled with joy. This was better than any trophy he ever won or any autographing occasion in the past.

No wonder Brenda was dedicated to teaching. His class today had been a wonderful experience.

Then Alexander had a revelation which made him whistle in surprise. He had never cared for babies or little children. Had never been around them. But, now, he wanted someday, to have a teenage son—like the ones he met today. The logical lead-in to that occurrence was to find a wife who would become the mother of the longed-for son.

Getting married and having a family would fill the empty space in his life which had been plaguing him. This emptiness had increased since spring. There had to be more to life than selling and designing cars. Since his father's retirement and his parents' move to Europe, the house was lonely. It was no wonder he

The Tycoon and the Schoolteacher   113

spent so much of his time at his drafting table or in the garage.

He tried to imagine having a woman in his life all the time. To have her waiting for him to come home each night. To hold her in his arms while they lay in bed. To kiss her good morning. To never be alone, day or night.

He had met many women and still never found the right one.

Or had he finally . . . ?

He thought more about having a son. Brenda would probably tell him he was being politically incorrect. Why not think of having a son or a daughter? She was right. He had to give her the credit for making him think along different lines. First, about his cars and now about his personal life.

Though he had been stimulated by his contact with Brenda's students, he knew he would never be able to do what she did all day. Since the excitement and high of the class was wearing off, he felt emotionally drained.

Did Brenda feel this let-down at the end of her day? Every day? Or was she made of sterner, stronger stuff? He remembered the papers she said she had to correct every night. So her day didn't end at four o'clock.

Teaching was too draining a career for a petite person like Brenda. She should think of changing careers. Then he winced, remembering her reaction to his presumptuous remarks at the end of the farewell dinner.

*   *   *

114 *Ludima Gus Burton*

For two weeks after his teaching session on cars, Alexander wasn't able to contact Brenda. Her phone rang and rang. Her answering machine didn't pick up. Remembering her principal's unfriendly manner, he couldn't call her at the school. He made one more attempt on Thursday night. When he got her machine, he almost dropped the phone. Not as good as talking to her, but better than before. He invited her to dinner and asked that she contact him at the office.

No call came on Friday. He worked on reports after everyone left. An empty house didn't appeal to him. Before he left, he checked his answering machine. The message had come while he was out of the office for ten minutes.

"Have to chaperone. Take a raincheck on your invitation. Sorry. Brenda."

So he had missed her. Alexander groaned. Chaperone again. Not another dance. Well, he could endure it if she could. He'd go right now. They had time to have dinner before the dance. It wasn't what he had planned, but it would do. They'd be together.

Alexander's Camaro slid into the reserved parking space of a tenant. His hand out to ring the bell, the front door opened. Surprised, Brenda gave a shriek.

"Goodness. Where did you come from?"

"I got your message. I'm here to take you to dinner. Afterwards, I'll help you chaperone."

Brenda frowned. The king had spoken from on high. No "Please" or "May I?" or "Do you want my help?"

The Tycoon and the Schoolteacher   115

"Are you sure you want to come with me?" she asked and stifled a giggle. If he thought the dance was agony, wait until he suffered through tonight.

"Of course. Where shall we have dinner?"

"No time for that. I have to be at the school in twenty minutes."

"Why is the dance starting so early?"

"Dance? I never said that's my duty tonight."

"Brenda, stop being so mysterious. Tell me."

Chapter Eleven

"You're going on the fan bus to the basketball game with Jackson Central." She paused and then said, "It's an hour drive away."

"On a bus, a yellow school bus?" Astonishment almost chocked Alexander. His dismay deepened after his next question, "How many kids?"

"Well," Brenda dragged out her answer, "a full bus. Forty kids."

She peeked up at Alexander. She almost knew what his thoughts were. Forty? Forty? All on one little bus?

"Have you ever ridden on a school bus?" When he shook his head, she said, "You don't have to come with me. I didn't ask you; you invited yourself."

Alexander didn't answer her. He turned all his at-

The Tycoon and the Schoolteacher 117

tention to parking his car in a narrow end space. "Can you get out?" he asked.

"I think I can. I'll try not to scratch the door against the fence."

"The door be damned."

Riding in a crowded bus full of shouting kids scared the heck out of him. His closest contact with kids had been the fifteen in Brenda's class.

The bus was waiting for Brenda.

"Thank you for the ride," Brenda spoke over her shoulder and she started to board the bus.

"I'm coming with you."

"You can't. I was only teasing about you coming. Besides, only faculty—"

"I'm coming. Rules be damned."

Brenda shrugged her shoulders and greeted the bus driver. He gave her a big smile. "I won't tell." He gave Alexander the thumbs-up sign.

The bus load chorused, "Hello, Mr. Stone." One wise guy asked, "Are you going to be Miss Harrison's chaperone?"

"You better believe it. I'll see she behaves." The remark brought hoots of "That's the way to go, man!"

Brenda blushed. "We have to sit in the middle of the bus. It's not very comfortable."

She sat next to the window. Alexander's broad shoulders and hard thigh pressed against her in the narrow seat made for children.

Brenda, like the students, was wearing worn jeans,

an oversize Hilliard sweat shirt, and sneakers. Though it made her look adorable, it seemed hardly the attire for a chaperone. She appeared absurdly young and vulnerable, in need of being taken care of and protected.

Yet her principal expected her, a lone woman, to do the difficult job of maintaining discipline on this crowded bus. Evidently, Brenda accepted her responsibility as though it was an ordinary assignment. He was glad he came in case there was trouble she couldn't handle.

The bus started with a jerk. Alexander grabbed the back of the seat in front of him to keep from falling into the aisle.

He growled, "Not only uncomfortable but damn near impossible."

He shifted closer to her and flung his arm around her shoulders. Tonight, Brenda's hair had been fastened away from her face with two combs. In the back it fell in a black waterfall. Its silken strands fell over his hand. He caught his breath at the soft touch.

"Mr. Stone has his arm around Miss Harrison," the watchdog in back of them announced to the whole bus.

"Yes, I do." Alexander raised his voice in a no-nonsense tone, "No more comments, you hear."

He learned his office authority carried no weight.

"Sure thing, Mr. Stone, anything you say," a familiar male voice answered. "You can hold her hand, but you can't kiss her. Them's the rule!"

The Tycoon and the Schoolteacher   119

A giggle ran through the bus. "Them's the rule," was shouted merrily.

Alexander looked down at Brenda. Her cheeks were a rosy red and she was dimpling up at him. He wanted to take her hand, as the kids said was permitted, but held back. He wasn't an adolescent boy—even though he wondered why his hormones didn't know that fact of life. Besides, he didn't want to give her principal any cause to reprimand her. As it was, he shouldn't be on the bus in the first place.

During the exciting game, Alexander found himself on his feet cheering the Hilliard team and yelling with the best of them until his throat was raw.

The game went into overtime. The din was so loud it was a wonder the roof of the gym didn't blow off. When Hilliard won, pandemonium reigned.

Alexander grabbed Brenda in a fierce embrace and swung her around, loving the sound of her yell. He put her back on her feet. The noise in the gym rivaled the roaring in his ears and the pounding of his heart at the electric shock consuming him.

A most intimate touch—

At the wrong time and in the wrong place.

Brenda's long lashes fanned her red cheeks and her lips parted. She wanted him—

Wrong place and wrong time!

Brenda turned quickly to Alexander.

"The bus is waiting for us," she said. She'd worry on Monday about the lecture her principal would deliver to her. She had seen him at the back of the gym watching her. He frequently found petty reasons to call her into his office.

On the bus, they couldn't talk because of the din of victory. "Ninety-nine bottles of beer on the wall" was started, to last all the way home.

"We sang that song in my school," Alexander said in the pink ear of Brenda. His lips were so close that he felt it was so close to the forbidden, against the rules, kiss. Had he made it a kiss, the event would have been broadcast to the whole bus. To eventually reach the ears of the principal. He had the feeling he was the person who made all the rules.

The last bottle of beer was just reached as the bus pulled up before the school.

"Good night, Miss Harrison, good night, Mr. Stone. Don't do anything we wouldn't do!" was the helpful advice given to them as they started toward Alexander's car.

"Tired?" he asked. Brenda had settled in her seat and uttered a deep sigh.

"Always, after a bus trip, on a Friday night. I usually collapse on Fridays as soon as I come home from school. That's my 'do-nothing' evening of the week."

"This job is too much for you." Alexander wanted to press his case but he could see that Brenda was too tired. He said no more and let her rest quietly the rest of the way.

Brenda closed her eyes. Her pupil load this year was

The Tycoon and the Schoolteacher   121

too heavy for an English teacher. It was only for a year. Who knew? It might be less than that if Mr. Haggerty made trouble about tonight. It was too bad he had taken a dislike to her. Just one of those personality clashes which had no known cause.

Alexander helped Brenda out of the car and up the stairs. He cursed the lack of an elevator. Brenda's steps slowed with each flight. He wanted to pick her up and carry her to the door. He didn't dare. By now he knew his independent writer wouldn't stand for it.

He gave Brenda a gentle push inside her door. "I had a good time tonight. Thanks for letting me tag along."

"Thank you for coming. I don't think you'll accept another chaperone job without learning first what it is!"

"I might. Try me." He urged Brenda, "Get to bed. We'll talk later, okay?"

Brenda nodded her head and Alexander closed the door. He listened to hear the bolts slide into place. He walked slowly down the stairs and out to his car.

Tonight had been an eye-opener. There was something wrong with a school administration that sent a lone woman on such an after-school duty. A male teacher should have been assigned with her. He was going to become more involved with the public school system, at least, Hilliard's.

He worried about Brenda. She was tired and this was still only the beginning of the school year. How could he persuade her to leave? Even as the thought crossed his mind, he knew it was impossible. Brenda was a fighter and would never quit in the middle of her contract. What she pledged to do, she would do. She did it with the book this past summer. He suspected she had worked on it at night. She even finished early. Now, he remembered the circles under her eyes and knew why they were there. He should have been more observant. But she was so good at acting bubbly and energetic—and those smiles! They made a dreary day bright with sunshine and cheered the cockles of his soul.

If he couldn't change her class workload, he could take her out to dinner, the movies, or for a drive on the weekends. Alexander's heart lightened with his plans to make Brenda's life happier.

Unfortunately, he had to put his plans aside. A car conference in Boston took precedence.

Brenda made her plans for the long Thanksgiving Day weekend. No school from Wednesday noon to Sunday night—heaven for sure. She planned to sleep late and do no school work.

She'd shop on Wednesday afternoon for her solitary Thanksgiving feast and not think about how much she missed her Aunt Margaret. Her aunt had made the holiday a special occasion with her little basket made from construction paper in yellow and brown with a small turkey on the side, filled with assorted nuts and candies.

The Tycoon and the Schoolteacher   123

She'd roast a small turkey breast and even bake a pumpkin pie after her aunt's recipe.

A lonely meal, but she wasn't going to get depressed, or think about Alexander, or long to see him. She needed to rest and not think of the evaluation report which would be waiting for her when the vacation was over.

What did Alexander do on Thanksgiving? His parents were in Europe. He did have his Uncle Charles. Such a nice man. How fortunate she met him at the Library Fund Raiser. It started a chain of events which was still going on.

For a reason she didn't want to pin her dreams on, Alexander was still in her life. The chaperone job on the fan bus must have cooled his interest. She hadn't seen or heard from him since that night. Of course, bus duty wasn't the easiest after-school duty to be assigned to, but she, perversely, enjoyed it. The kids were so happy—noisy, yes!—and carefree on the bus.

Thank heavens for her tenth-grade homeroom class with which she began and ended her long day. The rapport they had with one another was magical. Annie Murphy was the leader, with George Allen her able second hand. They loved to tease her about her "boyfriend."

"He's not my boyfriend!"

Her protests were ignored. All she could do was groan and throw up her hands in defeat.

As fate would have it, to prove their story, Alexander had to step sharply to the side of the doorway as the students whooped and hollered as they left for their vacation on Wednesday.

"She's all yours, Mr. Stone. Enjoy yourselves!"

"Will do. Thanks."

Brenda grasped her hands to still their trembling. She smiled at Alexander.

He grinned back and came to stand beside her. He took her hands in his, feeling the tremor in them. He squeezed a little tighter to reassure her.

"Hello," he said. "I've been out-of-town on business."

"I wondered what had happened to you." She let her hands lay in his warm ones.

Her answer made Alexander inordinately happy and encouraged. She had been thinking of him.

"Please have Thanksgiving dinner with me. Mrs. McAllister has it all planned."

Happiness unfolded in Brenda like the petals of a rose. No lonely dinner for her.

"I'd love to."

Alexander let out his breath. He had expected a refusal.

"Perfect. I'll come for you at one o'clock. Mrs. Mac wants to serve dinner at two. Okay?"

Brenda nodded her head and slowly withdrew her hands from his grasp. She shuffled a pile of papers into her briefcase.

Alexander frowned. "You're not correcting—"

"Heavens, no! As of this minute, I'm on vacation until Monday morning."

The Tycoon and the Schoolteacher   125

"Fine. Then I'll take you to Anton's for supper and the movies."

It wasn't a request but Brenda overlooked it. It was what she wanted to do. The beginning of a wonderful vacation.

The old Oscar winner, *It Happened One Night*, entertained them. It hadn't been colorized, for which Brenda was glad. She liked seeing the classics in their original black and white. It was better, however to have Alexander sitting beside her sharing the popcorn. Their hands touched and pulled away, to touch again . . . They laughed at the same parts. Alexander's arm around her shoulders was comforting and exciting.

Alexander was so relaxed—a different person—and no longer her employer. Was that the reason? Could they find common ground to bind them together after all? Time would tell.

Brenda felt shy walking up the broad steps to the front double doors of the mansion. Today she was going to see the inside of the house that had always fascinated her.

The center hall had black and white marble flooring with a thick oriental rug over the center of it. Before her was a spectacular staircase which divided at the landing. A crystal chandelier hung from a vaulted ceiling over the foot of the staircase. It threw rainbow prisms of color.

The dining room was to her left.

Alexander led her into the long drawing room at her right. It was a lovely room with a high-beamed ceiling. The windows were wide and rose from the floor to the ceiling. Deep cornices of rich, red velvet crowned their tops. Diaphanous white lace curtains were framed with velvet drapes. Between the windows were family portraits in heavy, ornate gold frames. Brenda wanted to examine them more closely, to see if Alexander had inherited any of their features.

A multicolored oriental rug looked worn before the deep, cushioned red velvet couches and chairs grouped before the huge stone fireplace. One back wall had bookcases with leather bound volumes cover to cover with some paperbacks. In the corners were glass-fronted cabinets filled with beautiful china and curios.

The room was saved from being cold and formal by the casual scattering of books and magazines on the footstool, end tables, and on the floor beside one worn chair.

A fat, black and white cat came toward Brenda, mewing softly.

"Hello, sweetheart." Brenda reached down and petted her head. "What's her name?"

"She was dropped off on the highway and found her way to the back door. She's called 'Kitty.' "

Alexander threw up his hands at the look on Brenda's face. "I know, no imagination at all. When

The Tycoon and the Schoolteacher   127

she proceeded to have a litter of four kittens, she became Kitty Mommie and so she is to this day, four years later."

Brenda picked up Kitty and snuggled her against her cheek. Kitty purred loudly. Alexander felt so would he if her cheek touched his— He stopped the thought in midair.

"She has the run of the house now. You heard it said that you don't own a cat; she owns you."

"How true." What a different slant this put on Alexander. "Was this true when your parents lived here?"

"Yes, Kitty took residence a year before my father retired."

When Mrs. McAllister appeared in the doorway, Brenda put down the cat.

"Come in, you two," the housekeeper said, "dinner is served."

Mrs. McAllister had out-done herself. Only ambrosia from the gods could have surpassed her.

During the dinner, Alexander kept the conversation on subjects which interested Brenda. He liked watching her animated facial expressions and her ready smile. She looked and acted happy. Desire to make her happy and carefree always swept over him. She looked so at home in his house . . .

"After such a dinner, let's go for a walk." Alexander took Brenda's hand. Though it was sunny, there was a nip in the air. Alexander buttoned her coat under her chin. "Don't want you to get chilled."

128   *Ludima Gus Burton*

Brenda nodded, unable to swallow the big lump that blocked her voice passage. It felt wonderful to be taken care of again. She remembered Philip had been solicitous of her welfare. Strange, to think of Philip today. She felt guilty to let his memory intrude into Alexander's day. She pushed the past into the back of her mind and firmly closed the door.

Brenda slipped her arm into the crook of Alexander's elbow and smiled up at him. He drew her arm close to him and captured her hand in his other hand, giving it a gentle squeeze.

Brenda made no attempt to draw away from him. When they walked past the buildings in the lower complex, Alexander asked, "Do you want to go inside and see the cars once more?"

"Yes, very much. I spent so many happy hours with them."

"You enjoyed working here, didn't you?" Alexander wanted reassurance.

"Some of the happiest months of my life," Brenda confessed. "It was more like indulging in a hobby than working."

"I'm glad. However, I made it difficult for you."

"In the beginning you did," Brenda admitted, "but it soon passed."

"You know I appreciate the work you did on the book. I should have taken you with me when I went to Europe. My parents wanted to thank you."

"No need for that. I only did what I was paid to do."

The Tycoon and the Schoolteacher 129

Alexander nodded his head and unlocked the door. Without the noise and voices of the mechanics in the garage next door, the building sounded hollow. Brenda was glad when the lights came on and chased away the shadows of the approaching dusk. The carpet muffled their footsteps as they walked down the center aisle.

He led her to the far corner to the blue Chandler roadster.

"Here's your car." He smiled down at her.

"Yes, oh, yes." She touched the hood. "I shall miss seeing it when I move away."

"Move? When? You didn't tell me—"

"Not soon," Brenda hastened to explain. "I mean after the school year. Probably the end of June. I'll be applying for a new position for next year." She took a deep breath. "I definitely won't stay on at Hilliard. One year is enough."

"That's a relief. Even I can see Hilliard isn't the ideal school. I only wish this was the end of the year so you'd be almost out of there."

Brenda agreed with him. "I'll be glad when the last day comes. If it wasn't for my homeroom, it would be hard to endure on a daily basis."

"Are those the ones who were in the class I spoke to?"

"Yes. You'll have to come back sometimes. They speak of you often."

"I'll do that. Just let me know when." He again had

the vision of a teenage son of his own. It wasn't surprising that the boy had black hair . . .

Brenda looked down to see Kitty Mommie brushing up against Alexander's leg. She reached down and petted her head. The cat immediately turned on her back and demanded to have her tummy stroked. Brenda complied. "She must have followed us."

"Don't be surprised if she goes with us for the rest of our walk. She's adopted you as a member of the family."

The evening was spent in front of the fire. Brenda, spying the beautiful ivory chess set, challenged Alexander to a game. It was touch and go most of the time until Alexander masterfully and with a loud shout of victory made the final conquest.

"I bow to you, my king," Brenda teased. Then she promised, "Until the next time. I'll win."

At her apartment door, Brenda said, "Thank you for having me share your Thanksgiving." She admitted, "I was feeling sorry for myself Wednesday morning."

Alexander unlocked the door and put the key in her hand. "You saved me, too." His gaze was warm. "Two lonely souls have to stick together."

"Sounds like a good idea. Good night and thank you again."

Alexander bent down and kissed her cheek. "Good night and pleasant dreams. Inside you go—and lock the door."

The Tycoon and the Schoolteacher   131

Brenda listened until Alexander's footsteps on the wooden stairs faded away.

Again, only a kiss on the cheek. She caressed the spot. A barometer of their relationship. So far, and no further.

She looked around her apartment. After the splendor of the mansion, every fault glared at her. It was more than the opulent furnishings and the size of the mansion. She had felt at home, as though she belonged . . . No, she had dreamed about it so much that it felt true. She appreciated his thoughtfulness today.

The light on her answering machine caught her eye.

Chapter Twelve

The message sounded urgent: Call Amy Webster, no matter the hour, at this number . . .

An unusual request. Philip's mother had hated her and done everything to break up the relationship. Brenda felt she would have done it to any woman— no one was good enough for her son.

The telephone message caused the past to come flooding back—the State Trooper appearing at the door, her rush to the hospital, the utter despair and disbelief that Philip was really dead. Tears pricked her eyelids.

The wound had healed and she had filled her dreams with Alexander. Though they were only dreams, they gave her hope that, someday in the future, a man would love her, that she would marry and have a fam-

The Tycoon and the Schoolteacher   133

ily. Until then, she visualized the physical form of Alexander as that man.

She didn't want Amy Webster destroying the fragile peace of her life. However, she would call—and had the malicious thought that an 11:30 call would wake her up.

Mrs. Webster's voice was as chilly and unfriendly as in the past. She wouldn't take "no" for an answer. Brenda agreed to take an early train to Simpson the next morning and meet her at the lawyer's office. All would be explained at that time.

Brenda sighed. A day of her vacation would be ruined.

She wanted to call Alexander and tell him of her plans. He said he would call her on Friday. True, no definite time was indicated. Still, she had the feeling he expected her to be there for his call.

She decided, instead, to call from Simpson at a reasonable hour.

When repeated calls to Brenda, Friday morning, brought only the answering machine message, Alexander gave up. He was hurt and disappointed. He had been sure the good time they had had together yesterday would be repeated on Friday and the rest of the weekend. He had been mistaken. His frustration was keen. No other woman had treated him in this manner. He had to accept the fact that Brenda had no real interest in furthering a relationship. With Brenda, it was one step forward and two steps back!

He accepted his uncle's invitation to fly to Florida for a golf weekend.

What with so many startling things happening, it was late afternoon before Brenda called Alexander.

Alexander hadn't waited. So much for thinking their relationship had reached a higher level.

She was rich.

She couldn't believe it.

Philip had put her name, jointly with his, on the deed to the weekend cottage they had looked at. Was it to have been a wedding present to her? At his death, his mother inherited the other half. The property was vital to the construction plans for a resort complex. The company's offer was lucrative.

Brenda and Amy signed the bill of sale.

In a short time Brenda would be, in her estimation, a rich woman. How poignant it was to have a wonderful legacy of the love Philip had for her. There was no longer any doubt that he had loved her. His mother had been wrong. Her memories of his love would always be beautiful.

For the first time in her life she was financially secure. No more worries about school politics or tenure. It was heady stuff to realize she'd have an investment portfolio. She could even hand in her resignation to Mr. Haggerty and finish her graduate studies in day session at the college.

She shook her head. She was going to fulfill her

The Tycoon and the Schoolteacher 135

year. She needed this reference in her folder. She was gaining valuable experience. It would be foolish to throw it away and have it haunt her at a later date. She'd be teaching for many more years. Old habits of being cautious won over her delight in her sudden wealth.

By the time Monday came, Brenda's euphoria had simmered down. What she had inherited was a small amount compared to the Stone wealth. The differences between Alexander and herself were there as much as in the past. A few dinners together, and the dollars now in her savings account weren't significant to change the reality of life.

During her free period on Monday, Brenda answered Mr. Haggerty's summons. He handed her his supervision evaluation of her teaching.

Brenda seethed. He had given her the lowest point value in all phases of her teaching. She read it through twice. She handed it back to him in silence, keeping a tight rein on her anger at the blatant unfairness of it. Then she remembered the money. Confidence bloomed in her. She wasn't at the mercy of this man for a job.

"What happens now?" she asked in a quiet voice.

"I could easily replace you with my nephew, but, for now, carry on. I will expect you to work harder at improving your teaching skills in the areas I've indicated."

Brenda merely nodded and left the office.

136 *Ludima Gus Burton*

What a difference her fortune already made in her life. If this had happened a week ago, she would have been devastated and frustrated. Now she felt self-confident and filled with a sense of security. Even freedom from fear. No wonder Alexander strode through life with his head high and lorded over all he surveyed.

The money made her feel like that, too. On a lower level, to be sure, but mighty heady, cloud-floating stuff.

"Improve her teaching skills?" Brenda thumbed her nose at the closed door of the office. Yeah. Sure thing!

Three-forty on Friday afternoon found Alexander entering Brenda's classroom.

"Your boyfriend's here again," Annie sang out.

Brenda's heart gave a happy leap. No word had come from Alexander and she had convinced herself that it was all for the best. She looked up from the big snowflake she was cutting out of white construction paper.

"Hello," she said, smiling shyly at him.

Alexander left the doorway and walked to her desk. With a shock he heard what he had subconsciously been thinking.

"Why don't you kiss her, Mr. Stone?" came the advice of a young voice. A general chorus took up the chant.

"Not with you jokers watching!"

When the closing bell rang, the class exited the room, shouting their good-byes.

The Tycoon and the Schoolteacher   137

"I'm glad you came," said Brenda with conviction. "Now I can stay late and finish these window decorations." Seeing the question mirrored in Alexander's eyes, Brenda explained, "I know it's only done in the elementary grades, but I find the high school students have a secret liking for them. My windows will be the only ones decorated in the high school but I don't care."

Alexander sat down by her work table, willing to wait until she was finished.

Brenda pushed a sheet of paper and a pair of scissors toward him. "You can cut out this snowflake for me. Just cut along the lines of the pattern."

Alexander looked aghast at the intricate design. Brenda made it sound like it was the easiest thing in the world to do. How was he going to manipulate these large scissors in all those tiny places?

"Damn," the frustrated oath burst out a few minutes later.

"Would you like to give up—"

"No. I can do it."

Brenda reached over and put her hand on his. "If you hold the scissors this way . . ."

Her touch made him almost drop the scissors. He wanted her to keep on helping him. "Show me again," he said.

"Just a little longer," she agreed. "There, you're getting the hang of it."

He kept on, his lips pursed in a determined line and his eyes intent on the sheet of paper. "I'm done," he announced with pride, not seeing the places he had missed or the ragged lines of the edges.

"That's wonderful," she praised him, thinking how endearing he looked. "I'll put yours in the middle window."

He kept watching in wonder and admiration as Brenda worked her magic with the other decorations. She alternated the windows with snowflakes and big, fat, red candles on a bed of green holly leaves. The last rays of the afternoon sun shone through the colored paper and made the room come alive. A Christmas tree paperweight rested on the corner of her green blotter with red corners.

"You're into Christmas, aren't you?"

"Yes indeed. I decorate my apartment early so I can enjoy the lights and decorations." She put away her supplies. "What do you do at the mansion?"

Alexander shrugged his shoulders. "Wreaths on the doors and poinsettia plants around . . ." He announced without preamble, "I won't be in town as I'm going to spend the holidays with my parents."

Brenda's heart plopped like a stone in a pond. She made a sudden decision. "I'm not going to be here, either. I'm spending my vacation in New York City with an old college friend." She crossed her fingers behind her back for telling the lie. She'd go to New York—alone.

"That's good." Relief filled Alexander. "I wondered what your plans were. You'll enjoy New York City."

Even as he enthused about the Big Apple he re-

The Tycoon and the Schoolteacher   139

gretted he wasn't going to be the person to show it to her. He could easily imagine her delighted cries and sparkling eyes. In fact, he wanted to show her the world . . .

Tonight was good-bye until after the New Year. Wise not to have an intimate dinner.

"How about Chinese tonight?"

"I'd love it."

Brenda slipped into her coat. Better to say good-bye in a noisy, brightly lit, Chinese restaurant.

A week later Brenda hurried past the Grant Men's Store. Out of the corner of her eye she saw the sweater on display. She did a double take and came back to the window. The pullover sweater was a beautiful bright red, a downy wool that would feel so soft. She pictured Alexander wearing it and saw herself held close in his arms as he kissed her under the mistletoe. She would lay her cheek against his heart and hear it beating with happiness because she was there, never to leave . . .

Though calling herself all kinds of a fool, she bought the sweater. This was the Christmas gift she wanted to give to him. But clothes were too intimate, especially when they touched his skin like a caress and looked so great on him.

She put the sweater in a box and slammed the drawer shut. She'd never give it to him.

Instead of the sweater, she mailed a gold key ring with his name engraved on the square plaque to his house. He wouldn't get it for Christmas but—it was the thought which counted, wasn't it?

Brenda's gift to Alexander was included in the box being forwarded from the servants. He was surprised and enormously pleased to find it. He put it under the artificial Christmas tree which was out-of-place with the palm trees outside the open window. Alexander experienced acute homesickness for a snowy Christmas in Canfield—or New York City.

The anniversary book was prominently displayed on the coffee table. He had caught his mother looking intently at the title page, her finger running over the name of the author. He wondered what she was thinking.

Brenda had bought him a gift before she knew he had chosen one for her. She had been thinking of him. The warm feeling filled an empty space in his heart. Spending Christmas in Europe wasn't so bad after all.

Even though she missed Alexander, Brenda enjoyed every minute of her vacation. Her hotel reservation was at the Marriott Hotel on Times Square, in the center of the action. The hotel also arranged tours and had tickets to any shows she wanted to see.

The vacation started on December twenty-second. When she got home, a messenger from Argosinger Jewelers delivered a long and slender package wrapped in shiny red paper with a big gold bow on it.

The Tycoon and the Schoolteacher   141

The card's message was simple: Merry Christmas, Brenda. From Alexander.

He hadn't forgotten her.

Brenda's joy filled her heart. Though she was tempted to open it immediately, she didn't. Instead, she planned when to do so.

She knew many adults opened their gifts on Christmas Eve. Twelve midnight in Europe would be 6:00 in the morning in New York City—practically at the crack of dawn, but she didn't care.

She'd open his gift at 6:00 and pretend they were together. Childish play, she knew, but so what? It was too bad her gift wouldn't be opened until he came back.

Though Brenda went on shopping sprees and packed in tours and shows, from early morning until late at night, she was horribly lonely amidst the holiday crowds. She wished, oh so desperately, that Alexander was with her.

Though it was still dark, at six, Brenda opened Alexander's gift. It was a slim gold bracelet with a delicate rose design engraved on it and a single diamond in the clasp. Its elegance took her breath away. She felt Alexander had taken time to select it. It wasn't a gift he might have given to any of the women in his past. It was for her alone.

Going to the window, she faced Europe. She flung out her arms and cried, "Alexander, your gift is beau-

142 *Ludima Gus Burton*

tiful and I'll always treasure it. I only wish I could thank you in person. I miss you so."

She dropped her arms and closed her eyes. She sent her thoughts into the ether waves, willing them to reach Alexander. Who knew? Maybe he'd think of her at the same time, their spirits in tune with each other.

Brenda put on her bracelet and kept it on, even in the shower.

At 12:00, Christmas Eve, Alexander felt driven to open Brenda's gift. At first glance it was an impersonal gift. A key ring with a gold square. He slipped it over his finger and swung it to and fro. The light fell on his engraved name on the square. No, Brenda had put thought into this gift—one which he would carry with him every day.

A bizarre feeling came over him. He closed his eyes and pictured Brenda opening his gift. They should have been opening their gifts together instead of being thousands of miles apart.

Strange, she felt so close . . .

Chapter Thirteen

On the Friday night of the third week of January, Brenda pulled the stack of semester test papers toward her. She'd have to spend the weekend correcting them.

Christmas vacation had come and gone as though it hadn't happened. Her days in New York took on the aura of a dream. Only when she wore the new clothes of her shopping spree did she believe it.

Alexander hadn't called and she had too much pride to call him. She wore the bracelet every day. Since it was slim, it didn't draw attention. She liked wearing it; it brought Alexander into her daily life. Worn on her right wrist, she looked at it often as she wrote.

Tonight she touched the bracelet. Perhaps it would

144   *Ludima Gus Burton*

work a miracle and help her correct more than one set
of papers.

The knock on the door startled her. She looked
through the peephole. Alexander waved to her. Happiness coursed through her.

She flung open the door.

"Hello," she said and wondered if this was the only
word in her vocabulary.

"Hello." Alexander smiled broadly and took her
hand. The bracelet caught his gaze and his heart
missed a beat. "I hoped you'd like it."

"It's beautiful. I wear it all the time." Too late. She
didn't need to make that admission.

He held up the key ring with his keys on it. "I use
this all the time, too."

They looked at each other and tension simmered
between them. Neither wanted to put it into words.

"Come in," Brenda urged. "Overlook the mess.
We've been busy giving tests and I have to get mine
corrected this weekend."

Alexander quickly glanced over the small studio
apartment he was seeing for the first time. He saw how
crowded it was with furniture and books and books
and books. Test papers were on the counter which separated the tiny kitchenette from the rest of the apartment.

His heart ached that she had so little space to live
in while he had rooms and rooms. Yet he could see it
was a cheery place with gay curtains, bright slipcovers on a sofa bed and armchair, and green plants.

The Tycoon and the Schoolteacher   145

Brenda had made it a home and he was proud of her efforts.

He walked to the counter and while his back was turned, she quickly and quietly hid the framed photo of him. She then followed him and cleared a space on the counter.

"Will you have a cup of coffee or tea?"

"Tea, please. I have it often with Mrs. Mac."

"I like it better than coffee at night," she said. "Sit down. It'll take only a minute to brew."

Alexander took the stool and casually looked at the top test of the stack. He saw that the beginning of the test was short answer questions.

"I could help you correct these if you have an answer key," he volunteered. "I wouldn't be much help on the other part."

Brenda gave him the cup of tea. "Milk? Sugar? Lemon?"

"Nothing. I like mine straight—the stronger, the better."

"I do, too." Brenda was delighted to find another thing they agreed on. "My Aunt Margaret came from England. It took her a long time to accept tea bags. On Sunday she'd treat us to a real pot of Earl Grey with homemade scones and tea cakes."

Alexander reached for the papers. "Shall we get to work?"

Brenda gave him the key to the answers and a red pen.

"Put a check mark in front of the wrong answers,

146 *Ludima Gus Burton*

add up the total on each page and place the number in the top left-hand corner."

She stood at his shoulder. Her hair hung down, disheveled and wild. It swung against his cheek. Her perfume, mixed with the scent of magic markers used to write the final test mark on the paper, made him want to put his arms around her. She was dressed in jeans and a sloppy T-shirt which proclaimed *Virginia is for Lovers*. Virginia? He was for lovers—correct that—one lover.

Brenda moved across the counter from him. Alexander looked up from the paper he was correcting. The adorable woman chewed on the end of the marking pencil, a little frown between her lovely eyes as she tried to make a decision about the essay before her.

She gazed into Alexander's eyes and quickly looked away.

"I have a question about this answer."

Brenda gave him the correct answer.

Five minutes later, Alexander said apologetically, "I need help on this paper. How do you read this chicken-scratch?"

"Lots of practice!"

"Sit next to me," he said a few minutes later. "I need help. I want these kids to get all the credit they deserve."

Sitting next to him would be hard, Brenda knew. She'd have to keep her thoughts on the papers instead of on him.

The evening wore on. Eyes became tired and bleary,

The Tycoon and the Schoolteacher   147

muscles in the neck and shoulders became tight and tense, and the pile of papers grew smaller. Electricity flowed between them as they talked to each other, debated marks, touched hands, and rubbed shoulders.

"Sorry . . . is this the paper you wanted . . . take this pencil . . . here, let me do that . . ."

When Brenda wearily rubbed the back of her neck absent-mindedly, Alexander called a halt.

"Look at the time," he said, and took the marker out of her hand. "No more for you tonight." He ignored her cry of protest. "You got a good start and you'll finish in time." He urged, "Just call me for help and I'll come running."

Brenda gave a weak smile. She dearly loved the idea of calling him, but knew she wouldn't. She had made it a rule to never ask for help. She was fully capable of doing what needed to be done, be it disciplining her big high-school students or correcting an almost impossible stack of papers—or resisting his charm. He wasn't to know that the correcting process was only the first step. Grades had to be averaged, semester marks determined, and marks put on the report cards. Still, a start had been made tonight.

"Thank you so much."

"My pleasure. Well, not really. You must love teaching to put up with this phase of it. Personally, if I was in charge of the schools, I'd hire clerks to do this for the teachers. It would be so much more efficient and it would free up your time to just teach."

Brenda threw her hands up. "Alexander, do you

know how much that would cost? Schools are on tight budgets which are dependent on tax-payer dollars. There are no profits rolling in as you have in your business." She shook her head. "You just don't understand—"

"No, I don't, apparently, but I won't argue with you. You need to get to bed."

He placed a gentle kiss on her cheek. The door closed behind him. She shot the dead bolt, knowing he would wait until she did so.

Again, a kiss on the cheek. Another memory to savor and tuck away.

After tonight, would Alexander have a greater appreciation of her chosen career or less? He was critical of the paperwork and was ready to reform the system—with no thought of the cost. Of course, he never had to worry on that score. Still, she hoped he'd gotten a different perspective tonight.

Brenda cut out the red hearts and the fat cupids with their bows and arrows to put on her windows. Her class had told her, in no uncertain terms, that they didn't want to exchange valentines.

"Miss Harrison, you got to remember we're in high school. We exchanged valentines in third grade."

"Okay, okay. But Valentine's Day is celebrated by adults and not just little children."

"Yeah, well, that's different."

She went down in defeat, but she still made valentine cookies for them. They didn't object one iota.

The Tycoon and the Schoolteacher 149

* * *

After he helped to correct the papers, Alexander had called a number of times to find out how she was.

He explained he was busy working on his car for the April competition. She wished he had asked her to come and see its progress, not that she would have understood the mechanics. Still, it would have been wonderful to stand beside him, to be with him, to encourage and praise him. It didn't take much to make her feel happy . . . She missed going to the Stone Estate.

She would have to get over feeling empty and lost, all because she had been fool enough to fall in love with a man who would never love her.

Yes, she was in love, foolishly and impossibly, with Alexander. She had fallen in love with him that day long ago in June. His blond beauty had taken her breath away. Her Greek god Apollo had come to life in the golden bronze body of an American car racer and designer.

Still musing on her confession of love for Alexander, she was thrilled and surprised to hear from him.

"Have dinner with me," he urged. "Tomorrow night at seven—okay?"

Valentine's Day—did he know it?

"I'll expect you."

At the Castlerock Restaurant the love songs of the '30s and '40s were played softly by a small band. A Valentine bouquet was in the center of the table.

"You look lovely tonight," Alexander said, admiring the red dinner gown which accentuated her dark beauty. "Perfect to celebrate this special day."

Brenda's blush of pleasure made her even more beautiful in his eyes.

Small talk dominated the dinner conversation.

"Come, dance with me," Alexander asked.

Brenda went into his arms and he held her closely. Her perfume tantalized him and his lips kissed her forehead. She sighed in his arms and wished the night would never end.

She thought of the Valentine gift she had for him in the apartment and was glad that she had given in to the temptation to buy it.

"Please come in," Brenda urged Alexander before he had a chance to leave immediately.

Alexander looked around the small apartment and wanted to take Brenda away from it. He sat down on the sofa, conscious of the fact that she would be sleeping there soon.

Brenda handed him a package wrapped in red and white striped paper. Red ribbon, with white hearts imprinted on it, was tied around it.

"Happy Valentine's Day," she said, and waited for his reaction.

IIc surprised her by reaching into his breast pocket and pulling out a small, square package also wrapped in red. A heart pin, with an arrow through it, was on top. He handed it to her with a smile.

The Tycoon and the Schoolteacher   151

"Happy Valentine's Day," he said.

They looked at each other and then burst into peals of happy laughter. Their planned surprise had boomeranged.

Brenda sat down beside Alexander.

"You first," he insisted. She had been pleased with the bracelet and he hoped he had made the right choice again.

She carefully inserted her nail under the tape and folded back the paper without tearing it. Inside the velvet box was a gold filigree rose lapel pin.

"Do you like it?" he asked anxiously. "If it had been a real rose it would be red."

"It's lovely. I'll wear it often." She didn't dare to believe the message a red rose was supposed to signify. He probably meant to send a simple romantic thought on this day of romance. Of course, on Valentine's Day, red roses were popularly presented.

"Your turn," she said, keeping the box open and glancing at the rose from time to time.

He untied the ribbon and tore the paper off. Brenda smiled, thinking how differently a man unwrapped a gift from a woman.

The History of the American Sports Car, Alexander read the title out loud. His face lit up like a spotlight. "How did you ever find this book? It's been out of print—"

"I have a wonderful book seller who is a marvel at finding rare books."

152 *Ludima Gus Burton*

"This is . . ." his voice trailed off as he leafed through the book and became lost in its pages.

Brenda was happy to watch him.

Alexander suddenly looked up and apologized, "Sorry."

"I'm flattered you like the book so much."

"The best gift I ever received."

He got up and walked over to her. He gently pulled her out of the chair, put his arms around her, and kissed her.

His lips were warm and firm upon hers. His arms held her against him. He only ended the kiss when his lungs cried out for air. He looked into her eyes for a long moment.

"Oh," breathed Brenda, a dazed look in her eyes.

Realizing what he was starting, Alexander let her go.

"I better leave now," he said.

He picked up his book, the wrapping paper, and the ribbon. "Good night."

"Good night."

She leaned against the door. Mixed feelings filled her. She was puzzled at his abrupt departure—even a little angry at it. Then, she began feeling bemused and ridiculously happy for his beautiful gift.

Another thought struck her. Would he look at the wrapping paper and notice that "I love you" was printed again and again in the white stripe? And what would he think?

Or do?

The Tycoon and the Schoolteacher   153

These questions danced in her head only to be pushed aside by a more important fact.

Alexander had kissed, really kissed, her—on the lips. It had been thoroughly satisfying and made her want more. She ran her finger lightly over her lips. She closed her eyes and relived the moment.

She got into bed and slid the velvet box beneath her pillow and refused to berate herself for being foolish and absurdly young.

Alexander discovered the love message on the paper.

The message and the memory of the passionate kiss suddenly confused him. Had he been encouraging Brenda to think he was serious about her? True, he found her intriguing and interesting and very different from other women in his life. True, he felt drawn to her and kept going back to see her. The kiss tonight had stirred him to the depths, but it was only one kiss on the lips. His heart was not—was not—involved in any deep emotion for her. He did not love her.

He would stay away. And he knew he was running scared.

Chapter Fourteen

The smell of paint permeated the air in the hall.

What is Brenda up to now? Alexander waited for the door to open. His determination to stay away lasted a mere week.

"Coming," Brenda called out. "I'll be there in a minute."

There was no question what Brenda was up to—she was in the middle of a paint job.

Her hair was shoved under a dilapidated painter's cap, its peak askewed. The large sloppy T-shirt had at one time been white; now it had many colors of paint, in layers in some places. It was also used as a wipe cloth for painted hands. Her ragged jeans had been cut off very short, one leg shorter than the other. Her long

The Tycoon and the Schoolteacher   155

bare legs were splattered with white paint. Paint-splattered moccasins were on her feet.

"I don't know whether you should come in," Brenda said, a paint brush in her hand. "You'll get paint on your suit."

She pushed a tendril of hair off her cheek and left a smear of white paint. She asked pettishly, "Why are you wearing a suit? Isn't your office closed on Saturday?"

"Not for me," Alexander retorted defensively. "Fine with me if you don't want me to come in." He turned on his heel and left her standing in the open doorway.

"Well," she said to the air, "you didn't have to leave. All I did was ask a legitimate question."

Brenda went back into the living room and finished painting the inner wall of her living room. Her furniture had been pushed into a heap and covered with an old sheet. Newspapers covered the floor near the wall.

She made a pot of coffee. She wasn't going to think about Alexander. He hadn't called or come near her for a week. Evidently he had discovered the "I love you" on the wrapping paper and been scared away. That was okay with her. She never expected him to return her feelings. She, of course, would love him forever. She was glad he didn't stay today. He'd just be in the way. She was sure he had never held a paint brush in his hand.

The doorbell rang.

Alexander swaggered into the room. He had on his

old jeans, a T-shirt, and sneakers which had seen better days.

"Why are you painting only one wall?"

"Since I don't have any trees outside my apartment window, I'm painting some trees, grass, and flowers on the inside."

Brenda narrowed her eyes as she looked at the blank white wall. "I'll have blue skies and a hint of a gorgeous sunset."

"You're full of hidden talents. You never cease to amaze me."

"I minored in Art in college," Brenda informed him. "I also taught Art instead of having study-hall duty at Simpson Central School."

"Let me help you. I'm sure I can. I cut out your snowflake."

"I accept your gracious offer, sir. I'll get some paint for you." She stirred a bucket of paint. "You can help me with the background. I'll paint the sky and you can paint the green grass in the area below this line."

Alexander took the brush Brenda handed him. He had never painted before, but he knew he could do it. After all, how hard could it be? He straightened his shoulders and dipped his brush in the paint as Brenda was doing. He gingerly began to paint.

Brenda was painting in the blue sky with broad, sure strokes. She looked down from her perch on the step ladder. Paint was running down the handle of Alexander's brush and over his hand. She tossed a rag to him. "Here's a rag. Wipe the paint off your hands."

The Tycoon and the Schoolteacher   157

Alexander pursed his lips in determination. He wouldn't let this slip of a woman intimidate him. He would paint that dratted grass if it killed him. The green paint persisted in running down his arm, on his jeans, and into his sneakers. Looking down, he hoped Brenda wouldn't notice what seemed to be as much paint on the floor as on the wall.

Alexander worked in total silence and the torture went on. Slowly, drip by drip, blue paint dribbled down on his hair, his forehead, his cheek, and ended on his T-shirt.

"Oh, I'm sorry, Alexander," Brenda apologized. "I wasn't watching what I was doing. There's a clean rag on that chair."

Another blob of paint landed on his arm.

"Sorry, again. I must be reaching out too far." And she looked contrite and innocent.

As more paint landed on him, a drop here, a drop there, Alexander realized Brenda was purposely doing it. He looked up at her from under his brows. There was devilish glee dancing in her eyes. He finished the grass and laid down his brush, his hands still sticky with green paint.

Brenda came down from the ladder. "You're finished. So am I. There's paint remover—"

Alexander put his green hands on either side of her face and pulled her toward him.

"Alexander, what are you doing?" Brenda cried.

"Brenda, this is in appreciation of your paint job—on me."

His mouth came down firmly on her lips.

Her knees turned to mush and she clung to him. She found it to be a satisfying kiss in response to the desire that had been intensely building all afternoon.

They pulled apart breathlessly. Alexander looked down at her face. Brenda looked up at Alexander.

What a sight they presented; Brenda with a clown's face of green and Alexander with a speckled face like a robin's blue egg. They roared hysterically until they were spent. Common sense asserted itself.

"Here's paint remover, Alexander," Brenda said. "Come into the kitchen and we'll both get rid of this paint." She snickered again. "We got as much on us as we did on the wall."

"May I come tomorrow and watch you paint in the trees? The key word is watch."

"Of course. You've been a great help. Come at twelve and I'll cook you a Sunday dinner to show my appreciation. Better take this old sheet to put on your car seat." Her eyes twinkled. "You have a little paint on your clothes."

The roast-beef dinner, climaxed with Brenda's special chocolate-pudding cake, left Alexander lazy and replete.

He unearthed the armchair and sank into it with a contented sigh. "If I always ate as much as I have today, I'd weight a ton in no time."

"Aren't you going to help me today?"

"No. I'll just watch and give you advice."

The Tycoon and the Schoolteacher   159

Brenda's painting fascinated him. Her strokes were sure and she didn't hesitate in her choice of colors.

At the mural's left, she painted a big maple tree with long branches extending to the right. Dark blades of grass took shape, as well as tiny violets. Shadowy purple hills were on a distant horizon.

Brenda had forgotten his presence in her absorption with her painting.

Watching her gave him pleasure. A realization struck him with frightening force. This lovely woman could interest him for the rest of his life. He quickly thrust the thought away. Though Brenda smiled warmly at him and welcomed his company, it didn't mean she had more than friendly feelings for him. A few kisses didn't necessarily mean anything to her. Forget the "I love you" on the wrapping paper. It wasn't even in her handwriting.

While he wrestled with his thoughts, Brenda finished the mural. She started to clean her hands. "What do you think?"

"You're up there with Van Gogh."

"Silly. But I'm pleased with it. I'll enjoy it for the rest of my lease."

Alexander pushed his hand through his hair. "Your year is passing in a hurry. I keep forgetting your job ends in June. What are your plans?"

"I'm sending out my résumés for several openings. I don't expect to hear from them right away. I'm not worried. I'll find a teaching position."

Brenda wished Alexander would say he was going to miss her, but he kept silent.

Alexander didn't know what to say. He didn't trust his feelings, didn't understand them. From the first day, Brenda had cast a spell on him. It was because she was so different, both in looks and ambitions, he kept telling himself. His heart wasn't involved. And that was as he wanted it. She would be gone before long and it was for the best. He didn't want Brenda to get any wrong ideas about having a relationship. The best thing to do would be to stop coming around, to distance himself from her company, as he had vowed to do weeks ago.

"I'm sure you'll find what you're looking for. Your qualifications are excellent."

Brenda hid her disappointment. It was as she had been telling herself—Alexander wouldn't miss her because he didn't love her.

Chapter Fifteen

Company business and final adjustments to his car kept Alexander from contacting Brenda. He didn't try to surmise how Brenda would interpret his absence.

His housekeeper stopped him on his way to play tennis one unusually warm April Saturday.

Brenda had called her the day before to ask for a donation of cookies to be sold by her class as a fund-raising project for the end-of-the-year class picnic.

Mrs. McAllister was happy to do so. "I love to bake," she told Brenda, "and I don't get much chance since Alex is hardly here to eat. He has me worried. All that office work and that restaurant food isn't good for him, if you ask me. And those late hours! He doesn't get enough sleep, either."

Restaurants . . . late hours . . . Alexander must be

161

having an active social life. He wasn't missing her. And she had been foolishly pining for him. No more!

"Can you have the cookies delivered to the Hess Station, the corner of 15th and 8th, by nine o'clock? I don't have a car any more or I'd pick them up myself."

Mrs. MacAllister told Brenda not to worry.

Mrs. McAllister smiled at Alexander. "You can do something for me on your way to the Club. I promised to have these cookies and cake delivered for a bake sale at the Hess Station. You'll do this for me, won't you?"

"Of course. It's on my way."

Alexander asked no questions. His housekeeper was always being asked to bake for the church. The Hess Station? He shrugged his shoulders and skillfully drove his car through the traffic.

His thoughts were on Brenda. Since he was always thinking of her, he was foolish to stay away. He'd call her tomorrow.

Shouts and shrieks could be heard a half block away. What kind of a bake sale was this? He saw the hand-lettered sign tacked to a pole: BAKE SALE AND CAR WASH.

He pulled into a parking space as far from the station building as he could get. Water from a hose could be seen arching into the air. The top of his car was down. He didn't want any accidental water to douse his leather interior.

The Tycoon and the Schoolteacher   163

He carefully lifted the five boxes of baked goods. His chin rested on the top box to steady the pile. He wondered why his housekeeper had donated so much. Alexander rounded the corner of the station house and started to walk to the girl whose back was to him, arranging trays of cookies. Beyond her was a group of kids energetically washing a car. They looked familiar. Brenda turned and saw him. Her mouth dropped open.

"Well," Alexander said as his heart gave a big jolt, "I don't have to tell you who's responsible for these baked goods."

Brenda's happiness spilled into her gaze and washed over Alexander like a tidal wave of joy.

There was no doubt of her welcome. Alexander almost dropped the boxes.

Her hair was in a pony tail and, again, she looked absurdly young. Her t-shirt, with its I LOVE NEW YORK logo, and short, cut-off jeans were wet from the car wash. She was more beautiful than he had ever seen her. Her beauty was a constant surprise to him. No matter what she wore or whatever situation he found her in, she captivated him in a new and deeper way. He felt as though he was in quicksand and going down fast.

Brenda looked at Alexander. He was in a spotless white silk sports shirt, white shorts, and sneakers. A tennis outfit. He was on his way to play tennis, probably with a beautiful blond. Brenda turned her back to

164 *Ludima Gus Burton*

Alexander. Well, let him go to her. She should have known he came only to deliver the baked goods.

"What do you want me to do?" Alexander's voice came at her shoulder.

He was going to stay, sang Brenda's heart.

The kids at the car wash spotted Alexander. They shouted to him, "Hi. You gonna help us wash cars?"

"Sure thing—after I help Miss Harrison."

"Why are you raising this money?"

"We plan to go to the Great Escape Amusement Park the last day of school. We hope to have enough to pay for admission and buy their food."

Two hours later, Brenda said with great satisfaction, "We've sold out all the baked goods." She added mischievously, "Let's go and help with the car wash. Look at that line of cars." She grabbed Alexander's hand and pulled him with her.

A minute later there was a splash. The water from Herman's hose doused them. Alexander sputtered and wiped the water on his face.

"Sorry, that was a mistake," Herman yelled.

"Sure." Alexander warned, "The day isn't over yet."

No one knew who actually started it, but, after the last car was washed, spontaneously the water hoses were turned on each other. A bucket of soapy water was thrown in Alexander's and Brenda's direction. They escaped by a fraction of an inch.

This was war. Annie and Charles joined Alexander and Brenda to do battle with the other side. Finally, a mutual truce was called.

The Tycoon and the Schoolteacher   165

Since the sun was disappearing behind the building, a chilly breeze played on their wet bodies.

"Get on home as soon as you can," Brenda called out. "I don't want you to catch colds." She praised them lavishly. "You all worked so hard and we've made a lot of money. A couple more sales and we'll have enough to pay for everything at the park."

They left with happy grins. Annie called out, "You're coming with us to the amusement park, aren't you, Mr. Stone?"

"I wouldn't miss it for the world."

When they were alone, Alexander turned to Brenda, "I've got to get you home before you catch cold." He reached into his back seat for the towel. He gently dried her face and dabbed at her hair. His hand touched her cheek and he caught himself from kissing her—

"Let's get you home," he said gruffly.

Before they arrived at her apartment, Alexander said, "I leave on Thursday for New York. My parents are meeting me there. We'll go together to the International Car Show."

"How time flies. You must be so excited about your entry." She smiled at him. "I know you'll get first place. Your car is truly wonderful."

A warm glow flooded Alexander to hear her words of praise. He opened his mouth to ask her to come with him to New York, but the words never came out. He lost his courage, fearing she would refuse.

He carried her parting words in his mind and heart.

"Good luck, and I'll be sending out my positive thoughts to make sure you get the recognition you deserve for your designs."

A week later, Alexander held the award in his hands and took a deep breath. He was alone in his New York hotel room. Suddenly, he was utterly weary. At last the strain was over and he could relax.

For a whole year the desire to make his mark in the world of sports car design consumed him. He wanted to be accepted for himself and his ability, not for his wealth or his past exploits in racing—he had the intelligence and creativity to make something no one else could do.

He had done it.

He should have felt satisfied, but he didn't.

With his parents at his side, he accepted the special award for "Uniqueness in Design," a His and Hers Special Edition XL.

He owed so much to Brenda because she had provided the initial idea on which the car was the final result. It had been her insistence that women also want to own a sports car—adjusted, for their comfort and safety, to be sure.

He had to see her and give her the credit due her when he got back to Canfield.

Brenda read in the *Canfield Times* about Alexander's award. She was so happy for him. He had worked hard for a year to achieve world acclaim for his design and practical applications. His dream had

The Tycoon and the Schoolteacher   167

come true. She hoped her encouragement on several occasions led to the happy result.

She looked forward to seeing the car in the Stone Showroom. Already the mayor was planning a ceremony to honor their local celebrity.

She stood at the back of the crowd at the celebration. She saw how Alexander's gaze swept the spectators, as though he was searching for someone. Suddenly he was gazing into her eyes and he smiled directly at her. Then a tall man stepped in front of her. When she was able to move to the side, the magical moment was gone.

He looked uncomfortable with the praise showered on him and accepted it all graciously and modestly. She was proud of him.

She didn't go to the front after the ceremony. Alexander was surrounded by well wishers and she felt shy.

She went home, feeling despondent and unhappy. She shuffled through her mail. A letter dropped to the floor.

A Texas postmark! A reply to her résumé!

She read through it again.

Chapter Sixteen

It had happened! Her dream was coming true years before she had expected it. She wanted to shout and dance around her crowded apartment, weaving in and out of the furniture.

Instead, she sank into her armchair.

Gifford Central School in Brainard, Texas, had accepted her application for principal, dependent upon her personal interview with the school superintendent on this coming Friday. They would pay for her plane fare and hotel accommodations during the weekend. She only needed to say she was coming.

She was going to be a principal.

Her night courses in the last five years to gain her certification in school administration had paid off. At last, she would be in a position of power to make

The Tycoon and the Schoolteacher 169

necessary changes based on her own classroom experience. She wanted to help teachers be able to teach, not be tied down with time-consuming administrative demands. Young people should get the best education in order to live in this difficult world. Good teachers were the answer.

After the first flush of joy, Brenda fell into a dreamy, reflective mood. It was easy to picture herself in the new role, behind a big desk, in a nice office. The years would go by and she would be looked upon as a remarkable, admirable administrator in the community she would enter as a newcomer and a stranger.

Years—living as a single woman, a spinster, an old maid!

That picture wasn't a happy one. Though she loved her career, she knew she never wanted it to consume her, to be her total life. Always, she dreamed of marriage to a man she loved, and who loved her, and of having children. Never would she be content to have only one child, to suffer as she had with loneliness.

Did Alexander plan to marry and have children? He didn't seem to be in a hurry to do so. He was in his middle thirties. A man, however, could wait, not take the first woman who came along.

A woman had a biological clock that kept ticking.

This line of thought led to another. Was this the reason for so many divorces? A woman, from fear, rushing into marriage. It probably was one of the reasons. She, for one, wasn't going to make such a mistake. No rushing for her. She'd marry a "forever love," a man who loved her.

She read the letter from Texas for the third time, still not quite believing it was real.

She wanted to tell Alexander about her good fortune. He'd celebrate with her. He wanted her out of the classroom because he thought she worked too hard. Yet she had a sinking feeling he didn't understand how much she loved the teaching profession and her intention to stay in it. She put aside all thoughts of Alexander.

A principalship would give her the best experience— she'd be able to have daily contact with young people, help teachers, and make improvements for the future. It would be so wonderful. She was almost afraid to be so happy, to annoy the gods . . .

While Alexander struggled with his feelings and hopes for his future, he stayed away from Brenda. Finally, realization came to him.

He was in love with Brenda and had been from the first day.

He loved her determination, her intelligence, her heart-warming laughter, her adorable smile, her eyes and lips. He loved everything about her. He was suddenly filled with a happiness he had never known before. He had found the woman of his dreams.

He couldn't wait a moment longer to pour out this truth to Brenda, and to beg her to marry him and make him a happy man.

The Tycoon and the Schoolteacher   171

*   *   *

The drive to Brenda's was a blur. He took the stairs two at a time. He knocked sharply.

Brenda's blue eye appeared in the peephole. He heard the bolt slide back and the chain drop. It added to his pleasure that Brenda was security conscious. He didn't want anything to happen to her.

"I'm so glad to see you," Brenda greeted him. Her smile enfolded him with warmth and brightness.

"I have something I want to tell you," he blurted out. He knew he should have invited her out to dinner and found a romantic place to tell her, but he couldn't wait. Surely she would understand.

"So do I," Brenda cried. Suddenly aware of his eagerness, she said, "You go first."

"No, you go," he said. "What I have to say may take time." Maybe not his words, but showing his love for her by taking her in his arms and kissing her again and again. How much time he had wasted and needed to make up.

"Read this letter," Brenda said. "I'm so happy. My dream has come true."

Alexander's heart landed at his feet. He wasn't going to be the one to make her dream come true. Reluctantly, he took the letter and read it slowly. He knew he had to say something quickly. Brenda was waiting for his congratulations.

"If this is what you've been dreaming about, then congratulations." When he saw the pain in Brenda's eyes as a result of his lukewarm words, he could have

172 *Ludima Gus Burton*

kicked himself. He never wanted to hurt her, ever.

"So this was the reason for your college courses. I made the wrong assumption that they were only required refresher courses." He gave a rueful smile. "I should have paid more attention."

"This year I completed the requirements for my certification. Being a principal will give me a chance to make a difference in the lives of my students. My experience as a classroom teacher will be invaluable. I never expected to become a principal so soon—thirty was my goal!"

She turned away to put the letter on the counter.

She hid her disappointment from his lack of enthusiasm. She had been so sure he would be happy, very happy for her.

"You came to tell me something," she said, "What was it?"

He changed his plans. No way could he ask Brenda to marry him today, not while her eyes were aglow with happiness at her principalship in Texas—miles away from him. His original plan to take her for an intimate dinner at a romantic place to make his proposal was best. The right time and the right place were essential if he was going to offset her news.

He answered her question. "It can wait. Have dinner with me tomorrow night."

Brenda lay awake for a long time. It still seemed like a dream and she couldn't quite believe the letter's contents were real.

The Tycoon and the Schoolteacher   173

If only Alexander had been happier for her. What had he really wanted to tell her? He had acted so excited, so bursting with exhilaration. That his invitation to dinner had been an after-thought, she was convinced.

Would she ever know the real reason for his visit today? If only she had made him talk first, as he had wanted to do.

"If only's" were a waste of time. If it was to be, she would learn soon enough the reason for Alexander's visit.

Having reiterated her life's philosophy, Brenda turned to her other side and, to her surprise, fell asleep.

They dined at their usual table at the Castlerock. She had bought a new blue dress which Alexander admired. As they dallied over their after-dinner coffee he looked at her intently.

"You're wearing your hair differently," he finally decided.

"It's called a Dragon's Knot." At his raised eyebrow she explained, "Instead of dividing the hair into three sections and braiding it, you divide it into two sections. Then you just tie a knot in it, again and again until the end and bring it up. I've used my grandmother's Spanish comb to keep it in place."

"Two sections? Hum. I think I could do that." It wasn't what he had in mind. He'd rather untie the hair to make it fall free.

After leaving the restaurant, Alexander drove with

174 *Ludima Gus Burton*

practiced speed out of town and up the winding road of the mountain. The car slid smoothly into the parking place at Lookout Mountain.

They got out of the car and leaned over the railing to look at the peaceful valley below. A crescent moon hung close to the horizon and brilliant stars filled the sky.

Alexander turned Brenda to him.

Gently taking her face in his big hands, he kissed her. And again. His hands left her face and his arms drew her to him in a close embrace. Her arms encircled his neck and her fingers tangled with his hair.

"Brenda, my darling, I love you, I love you." With his lips still brushing hers, he asked, "Will you marry me?"

"Oh, Alexander, are you s..s..sure? Do you know what you're saying?"

A hearty, wild shout burst from him. "Yes, yes, yes! Say you love me and will marry me."

"Yes, I'll marry you because I love you."

Later, it was time for words.

Brenda snuggled deeper into Alexander's embrace. She gave a contented sigh of happiness. She imagined their happy life together—he at his car dealership and she, teaching.

"What do we do now, Alexander?"

"We get married and live happily ever after," Alexander answered. "However, I do this first."

He tossed the combs aside and deftly untied the

The Tycoon and the Schoolteacher   175

Dragon's Knot, to free her soft hair about her shoulders. "Later, I'll knot your hair."

He didn't want to talk; he wanted to kiss her.

Brenda persisted, "What do we do now?"

"You resign your teaching position—"

"Wait a minute! Do you mean tomorrow?" Brenda pulled away from Alexander.

"Of course not. That wouldn't be professional. At the end of this year. Then we'll get married."

A cold feeling began to circle her heart at Alexander's imperious plan for her life. She dreaded asking her next question.

"What about my principal's job in Texas?"

"You turn it down. You won't need to work ever again after you become my wife." Alexander sounded determined and smug.

Brenda was speechless. Alexander had casually waved away her chance to attain her life's goal. He had demonstrated again his utter lack of understanding of what had been and still was important in her life. He expected her to give up everything she had worked so hard for. As though she longed for a life of ease!

"Let me get this straight. You expect me to give up teaching and being a principal in order to become your wife?" Brenda's question was uttered in a cold, even tone.

Alexander's eyes widened in surprise. He became conscious of the glacial air drifting from Brenda to him. In his happiness, he hadn't thought she might not agree with him. It had been obvious to him how the

176 *Ludima Gus Burton*

future was to unfold for the two of them. He wanted a full-time wife as his mother had been content to be. He had worried about the physical harm Brenda had been in when teaching at Hilliard. True, this year, there had been no real horror stories of student violence, but the possibility was still there. And Brenda was so petite—and fearless.

He remembered all too vividly her recounting the way she had waded in between two fighting students. She had laughed at her own fearlessness, saying, "They could have batted me against the wall as though I was a fly!" She had shrugged away his outraged concern. "It's all part of my day."

Brenda walked away from Alexander. She seemed miles away.

He pleaded, "Darling, think about it. Do you really want to be separated? You know I can't leave Canfield. If you go to Texas, we can't be married." He stretched out his hand and tried to draw her back into his arms, to kiss her into submission.

Brenda shrank away from him. Her heart was breaking. For one moment she had been in Paradise because Alexander loved her and wanted to marry her. Now, she was in the depths of hell because he expected her to make an impossible sacrifice, to give up her career and her dreams as though it was as easy as crumbling up a sheet of scrap paper and throwing it into a waste basket.

It wasn't Alexander's fault that she had, in her day-

The Tycoon and the Schoolteacher   177

dreams and besotted love, endowed him with perfect attributes and understanding. Her idol had feet of clay. No way did she want to marry this arrogant, egotistical, and domineering man. He would be running every aspect of her life and she would be ground under his ruling heel. He knew nothing, absolutely nothing about true love. What he felt for her was desire. Life with him would result in great unhappiness and dissatisfaction.

"I can't marry you, Alexander. I won't give up my dream of becoming a principal and you won't leave Canfield. Please take me home."

"Darling, please—"

"No. I don't want to talk about it any more. It's useless. We're miles apart. I knew it was too good to be true."

Alexander persisted after he started the car. "I love you and I won't give up."

Brenda didn't answer him. She kept looking out the side window of the car, seeing only the destruction of her world. She knew she would always love and long for Alexander, but he was asking too much. He hadn't voiced a possible compromise. As he hadn't understood her, neither had she, him. Two more mismatched people had never come together in this world.

How the gods must laugh at the foibles of lovers on earth.

At her apartment door, Alexander again tried to break through her defenses. "Brenda, my darling, we have to talk. We'll find a way out—"

178 *Ludima Gus Burton*

"Are you willing to have me continue teaching?"

"Well, I . . . Let's talk about it, but not tonight. You're too upset—"

"Yes, I'm upset," Brenda almost shouted. "Oh, go away, go away!"

She slammed the door and shot the bolt. She didn't answer his pleas. Finally, he left.

She cried herself to sleep.

The rest of the week was a blur to Brenda. She refused to talk to Alexander. After a while, he didn't call any more.

On Thursday she was surprised to be called into Mr. Haggerty's office. She wondered what his complaint would be this time. She was so glad she didn't have to put up with him after this year.

He surprised her.

"Miss Harrison, I've been observing you all year. You are a good teacher. I'd like to offer you a contract for next year. Mrs. Baird has resigned and her position is open."

Brenda gave a gasp. This was the last thing she expected. Because she didn't want to refuse until she was sure of her new offer, she stalled.

"I'm pleased and surprised at your offer. However, I have to see about rearranging my plans. May I give you my answer next week?"

"Yes," he said, unhappy with her reply. Brenda was sure he probably thought she would jump at the chance since positions in English were hard to find.

The Tycoon and the Schoolteacher   179

* * *

Friday, on the plane, Brenda decided she'd refuse Mr. Haggerty's offer. By staying in Canfield she ran the risk of seeing Alexander. She didn't trust her resolve to have nothing more to do with him. She was trusting distance to heal her heart.

Alexander was a very unhappy man. He missed Brenda deeply. He had never asked a woman to marry him. He found it hard to believe that this one woman, the woman he loved, had refused him. He had so much to offer the woman who became his wife: his undying love, social position, and a life of ease. He sincerely believed he could make a woman happy—make Brenda happy. He was even looking forward to having a teenage son; a baby was still impossible to imagine.

All day Friday, he prowled his office and barked at his employees. Brenda was accepting her principalship this weekend. In September she would be living hundreds of miles away from him. He resented her career which took her from him and was more important to her than her professed love for him. What a fool he had been to believe she loved him and wanted to marry him.

She did want marriage but only on her terms and her timetable. Marriage only after she had been able to be a principal. Sure, he realized this was her dream come true, but a whole year of waiting—and miles apart, at that. No, it was too much to ask any red-blooded man to endure. Not when she didn't need to work at all. She just didn't love him enough.

Brenda, Brenda, darling Brenda. He was never going to forget her. He was going to love her until the day he died. And he could never live without her—

Therefore—therefore—he had to change in order to have her.

He had been egotistical and selfish, asking a dedicated, ambitious, and hard working teacher to completely change her life for him. What he had to offer her was an empty social life. He had been thinking only of himself. If he loved her as he had told her he did, then he had to do all he could to make her happy.

He'd accept her need to teach wherever and whenever she wanted to do so.

The more Alexander thought, the more optimistic and happy he became. It was going to work out. He wouldn't stop trying until Brenda became his wife.

Brainard, Texas, enthralled Brenda. It was a western town out of the movies and books. It capitalized on using the western facades for the store fronts on the main shopping streets.

Her interview had gone well. The job was hers if she wanted it. The school was perfect. Yet, she hesitated and said she would give them her answer the following week.

Later, in the hotel, she didn't understand herself. Why was she hesitating? Before Alexander had said he loved her, she would have accepted. Before she had

The Tycoon and the Schoolteacher   181

only dreams about his love. It made a big difference to have it for real. To know she could be married to him, to live in his beautiful house, to have his children. To, finally, be supremely happy.

So why was she here in Texas, miles and miles away from the site of her dream husband, her dream house, and her dream family?

True, she would finally be a principal. It was her dream come true, wasn't it? But had she really given enough thought to this? For the first time, she wondered if she was too young to take on such a demanding job. Just having the credentials wasn't enough. She'd have to give up her personal life. And she loved teaching in a classroom and being in daily contact with her young students. An administrative job would distance them from her.

No, she wasn't going to accept the position. Having been offered the job was tantamount to achieving her goal.

Her heart filled with happiness. She was making the right choice. If only she could get on a plane this minute and hurry back to Canfield. This one time in her life she would call Alexander and not wait for him to call her. She was hungry for happiness and for love. They were tied up in the person of Alexander Stone, a man who had to hear her confession of love. This time she would ask him to marry her.

Alexander looked up and saw the light was on in Brenda's apartment. He had called Saturday night,

Sunday morning and afternoon with no success. On an off chance, he drove over tonight. After all, she had school tomorrow.

Taking the stairs two at a time, he rapped on her door.

Brenda still had her coat on and her suitcase was on the floor by the door. It had been a frustrating day for her with three delays in take-off because of sudden, violent thunderstorms.

Seeing Alexander, she flew into his open arms and kissed him hungrily. It was some time later that she threw off her coat and led him to the couch. She snuggled into his arms.

Alexander spoke first.

"Darling, I love you. I want you to be happy. You can teach all you want."

Brenda's wonder and joy lit up her face. Alexander had come to her and he wanted her to do as she pleased.

"Darling Alexander. You truly do love me." She took his face between her hands and kissed him gently. "I'm not going anywhere without you, especially to Texas. I made up my mind Saturday night. I can't bear to be separated from you either."

Alexander's whoop of joy filled the small apartment. Never had he expected a capitulation on Brenda's part so easily. It proved that they were on the same track and meant to be together. They were two parts of a whole.

It was not the time to waste in philosophical thinking.

He reached for her.

Epilogue

The organ swelled with the strains of the wedding march and the congregation rose to its feet. Alexander turned to watch his bride walk down the aisle on the arm of his Uncle Charles. Her radiant beauty brought tears to his eyes. He didn't deserve to possess this angel.

Her smile and the trusting love in her gaze were all he remembered of the ceremony.

They received the toasts for their happiness, cut and fed each other a piece of the five-tiered wedding cake, and danced the first dance at the reception held on the lawn of the mansion.

Alexander had been secretive of where they would be spending their honeymoon. Brenda didn't care. All that was important was to be together. She slipped upstairs to change into her travel outfit.

When she and Alexander came out the front door, they were again showered with rose petals.

Dodging the shower of petals, Brenda ran to the car parked before the door and stopped.

Alexander was opening the door of the 1926 blue Chandler roadster from the family collection.

"Oh, darling, you've made all my dreams come true. You remembered about my grandfather."

"I'll always be here to make you the happiest woman in the world."

Amid the cries of farewell from his parents, their friends, and her students, they drove away. The tin cans and old shoes tied to the bottom of the car bounced merrily. A JUST MARRIED sign on the open rumble seat proclaimed to the world the happy event.